HACKED

A Dark Horse Novel

J.S. SCOTT & CALI MACKAY

Hacked

A Dark Horse Novel

Copyright 2017 by J.S. Scott and Cali MacKay

Cover Design by Cali MacKay

ISBN: 978-1-946660-16-9 (E-Book)
ISBN: 978-1-946660-17-6 (Paperback)

CONTENTS

CHAPTER 1

Gavin

3:27 AM.

*T*he numbers on my alarm clock glowed neon in the dead of night as I shook off the dregs of my recurring nightmare and rolled out of bed, yet another night's sleep ruined. Rattled as I was, there was no point in trying to get back to sleep, and so I found myself, once again, staring into my bright computer screens, tapping away on my keyboard, and ignoring the very real fact that I had a problem that wouldn't go away—a problem that had been haunting me for far too long.

If I was going to be up, I might as well get some work done—and that meant working out the bugs in my latest program. It was a slight departure from the security work my tech company tackled, but had the potential to change the lives of those most vulnerable... the ones who fell through the cracks... the ones that others had forgotten... the ones even the Feds had a hard time tracking.

The dark web traded in blood and people's misery—*and I wanted to break its back.*

My business partner, Kane, thought I was insane to even attempt it, though he was happy to leave me to my hacking and my delusions. I knew there was a good chance the criminals might just burrow deeper, but I still might manage to save some lives in the meantime.

Like this one here...

I knew it was a hit of some sort, and though the details were sketchy and I hadn't figured them out yet—I *would* because *someone's life depended on it.*

After copying the ad and all the data associated with it, I eliminated the hit, but only after I managed to put up some smoke and mirrors, so that whoever put up the ad would still think it was active. That would buy me a little more time before they figured out that something had gone wrong with the post, and they'd have to put up a new one.

Though I didn't know when the hit might take place, the clock was ticking down for this person, since I had no doubt another post would eventually go up. The information was encrypted on someone's server, so I tweaked my code and ran it, hoping I'd get through the levels of security and find more information this time around.

And there it was... *a name.*

Charlie Wenham.

I didn't know what good ole Charlie had done, but someone had gone to a fair bit of trouble to put out a hit on him. Gathering what other information I could get off the post, I ran the info to see who I was dealing with, and why anyone would want them dead.

And... *that* was *not* what I'd been expecting. Because Charlie wasn't a *he*—he was a *she.*

Most definitely a she.

I groaned as my cock went hard at the mere sight of her. The girl was fucking adorable. There were a handful of pictures of her, though less than what one would expect from a woman in her mid to late twenties. There wasn't a whole lot of her on social media either—a birthday party at work, a picture of her with her dog, and a picture of her at a breast cancer run with a group of friends.

I couldn't keep my eyes from drifting to that last picture. Her long mahogany hair was in two braids, and she had on a hot pink tank top which showed off her generous curves. But it was her eyes, the color of candle-lit whiskey, and her hesitant smile that had me looking back at her, time and again.

Continuing my search, I couldn't find anything in her past or present that turned up any red flags for me. So then, why in the hell did someone want her dead? It didn't make any sense. This was not the sort of person people usually put hits out on.

I needed more time—time I didn't have—and more information. Because one thing was for sure—the girl would be dead before long if I didn't warn her.

With Thor in tow, I headed to the park just around the corner from Charlie's home, knowing that since she had a dog and seemed to be fairly active, there was a good chance she'd probably take her dog for a walk, especially since it was a gorgeous Saturday morning. Beyond that, I didn't know what the hell I was going to do, short of knocking on her door—which is exactly what I'd be forced into if my plan failed.

Yet I had no doubt that if I approached her and told her someone wanted her dead, she'd look at me like I was insane—and would likely think that *I* was the threat. But beyond casually running into her as a fellow dog owner, I hadn't a fucking clue as to what came after that. I'd just have to keep my fingers crossed that she'd show up at some point, and that I'd be able to charm my way into her life and find a way to keep her safe.

I groaned at the thought of having to turn up the charm, since I wasn't exactly the sort of guy who flirted with every woman I met—if at all. Though there was never any lack of interest from the women I came across, I tended to keep to myself, given my past. Not that I was completely anti-social. I couldn't be when Kane insisted on dragging me out of my hole and forced me to socialize—though that happened less often now that he was busy with Anna, and they were starting their life together.

Yet seeing Kane and Anna so happy together reminded me of all that was missing in my own life, and the truth was, *I wanted what they had.* I wanted to find someone to share my life with... someone to wake up with every morning... someone to share life's ups and downs. And though Thor was a great dog and technically fit the bill—someone a little less hairy and female was more of what I had in mind.

Someone I could fall in love with.

I got to the park bright and early the next day, not sure of her routine, and not wanting to miss her if she was the sort to get an early start to her day. Having already checked out the area, I positioned myself in the part of the park that was closest to her home, figuring she'd likely come this way. And in the meantime, Thor would get plenty of exercise playing fetch with his ball. He was still young and rambunctious, and had a tendency to get himself into trouble if he didn't burn off some energy.

Knowing that she lived alone, I was relieved to see she lived in a nice area, and as a scientist at a biotech company, she certainly had a decent job. But none of that would matter if I couldn't find a way to keep her safe.

I tossed the ball for a few hours, and was starting to think that I'd have to think of another way to "accidentally" bump into her, when Thor's ears perked up and a shepherd mix came bolting towards us, looking to play.

And wouldn't you know it... there she was, chasing after her pup. She caught up to it and grabbed the mutt by the collar, pulling her back. "So sorry about that. She's friendly—and usually she's better behaved."

"Don't worry about it. Nothing tires them out like playing with another dog. And Thor... he's so big that most other dog owners freak out about it, and won't let their dogs play with him. But honestly, he's just a big goofball. Wouldn't hurt a fly." I aimed for my most charming smile, hoping that I didn't look like an idiot.

"I'll admit, he's scary huge." She let out an adorable laugh as her eyes lit up, and I swear, I may have fallen in love—just a little. "I totally get it though. Ripley gets a bit of that, though she looks tiny compared to Thor—and great name by the way, especially for a dog that big."

I might be reaching with my guess, but she had on a vintage Firefly T-shirt, and I had a feeling... "Thanks. And... Ripley? It's not from Aliens, is it?"

"As a matter of fact, it is." Fucking hell, she had a great smile that made her eyes sparkle and come to life. "Color me impressed."

"I'm Gavin Reid by the way." So far, this was going a hell of a lot better than I'd expected.

"Charlie Wenham. My dad... he wanted a boy..." And just like that, the light in her eyes dimmed. But she shrugged it off, managing a bit of a smile as she tilted her head towards our dogs as they played and leapt around, trying to get one another to give chase. "Looks like they're having a good time."

"If Ripley can tire out that beast of mine, I'll be indebted to you." I stuffed my hands into the pockets of my jeans, hoping it'd kill the urge I had to reach out and touch her. No one had ever had this sort of effect on me before.

"Indebted, huh?" A blush crept across her cheeks, making her even more adorable. "I haven't seen you here before..."

I didn't want to lie to her, knowing that I'd have to tell her the whole story before long, and it'd bite me in the ass if I gave her *any* reason not to trust me. "I live about three towns over, but the park near us gets a bit crowded, and this one had great reviews on the dog park site."

"Guess that's not too far away to travel if it makes your dog happy." She shot me another charming smile, leaving me not only smitten, but wondering why the hell anyone would want her dead.

"He's so happy here, I might have to make this our new park." I'd happily make the twenty-minute trip if it meant getting to see Charlie again.

"I think Ripley would love that."

CHAPTER 2

Charlie

*M*eeting up with Gavin today made me wish I was the type of woman who could flirt and charm a man, so he'd be interested in dating me. Not that I had the slightest clue about how to lure a guy into asking me out. And up until today, the truth was, I'd never had the slightest interest in doing so.

For the most part, I lived for science and my research. They were a lot more interesting to me than attracting a man. Except that something told me this wasn't just *any* man.

For some reason, this particular guy was…*different*, and for the first time in my entire twenty-eight years on Earth, I wished I was more experienced at the whole dating thing.

As usual, I hadn't bothered much with my appearance. I'd braided my hair to keep the annoying mess out of the way. I wasn't wearing even a tiny bit of makeup. I never did. I was a science nerd, and spent most of my day in the lab working on my research. Nobody really paid attention to how I looked, and the men I worked with hardly noticed me unless I had something to say about a research project. And after a long day at work, I headed home to take Ripley out for a run.

No men.

Nowhere in my life.

And that had suited me just fine.

Until now.

I didn't know how to handle my instantaneous attraction to Gavin. He was handsome, and dressed casually, which only made sense if he was here to exercise his dog. He had on an old leather jacket over an indigo T-shirt, along with jeans that were lovingly worn and fit him perfectly, like they were his go-to pair.

With hair that was several shades of brown and blond, it was difficult to put an exact name to the color of his thick, cropped locks. His jaw was whiskered, like he'd been too distracted to shave for the last few days. Still, he *owned* the scruffy look, and that made him all the more handsome because he was confident without being pretentious.

By far, the feature that stood out the most for me was a pair of stunning, intelligent blue eyes that seemed to see into my soul.

And he liked my dog. How could I not like a guy who not only got along with Ripley, but who had a crazy mutt himself? Any man who didn't care whether his dog looked like a mishmash of different breeds and resembled a small bear with long fur had to be a nice guy, right?

"Was Thor a shelter dog?" I asked politely.

"Was it the impossible-to-determine mix of breeds that gave him away?" Gavin's blue eyes sparkled as he gave me an easy smile and casual shrug. "I've always liked the idea of giving something or someone a break when the odds didn't seem to be in their favor."

My heart skipped a beat as those beautiful eyes focused totally on me. "Well, if I had to guess, the odds *were* in Thor's favor the day you found him."

"I bet the same could be said about Ripley." Gavin sat down on one of the benches and waved at me to join him. I sat down at the other end of the bench as he continued. "I work from home, so I decided some company might be nice. I just wanted a normal sized dog, but I came home with a pony. He just kept barking at me, insisting I take him home—so I did."

I laughed because I couldn't help myself. He was pretending he was a pushover, which my instinct told me probably wasn't true. His gaze had been constantly moving before he'd focused on me, surveying his surroundings as though he needed to be aware of everything and everybody nearby. "He must have been so sad to be there, all cooped up in a kennel with little hope of getting adopted."

"Completely," Gavin said unhappily. "The poor boy looked absolutely miserable. He was overjoyed just to get a little attention, and I knew that very few people would consider a dog his size. I just couldn't leave him there."

"I think it's sweet," I argued. What kind of guy adopted the most pathetic dog at the pound? It's exactly what I'd done when I went to find a canine friend to bring home.

My adopted dog had been cowering in a corner all by herself when I'd approached her. One sad-eyed gaze and a few doggie kisses later, and she'd come home with me.

"Thor's still young, and his energy level wasn't really part of my plan, but..." Gavin shrugged and gave me another one of his charming smiles. "We manage okay, I suppose."

I couldn't help but smile back, feeling far more relaxed than I'd have expected to with a complete stranger—and a damn handsome one at that. "Do you plan everything?"

"For the most part, yeah. But sometimes other things take priority."

"I get that." I tended to be a planner myself, but sometimes things got derailed by surprises. "So... what kind of work do you do? Must be nice to able to work from home." I was curious to find out more about Gavin.

Even though he paid me plenty of attention, it was hard to miss that he was still watching his surroundings. I wouldn't exactly say he was nervous, but it was clear that he was well aware of anybody who came and went from the park.

"Internet security," he answered vaguely. "Nothing too exciting. Spend my day writing code, for the most part."

"So you keep people's information safe on the web?"

"Businesses mostly."

"So you're a computer geek?" I teased.

His smile widened. "Guilty."

"I'm a science nerd, so I respect that," I answered, starting to feel more and more comfortable talking to Gavin.

"What do you do exactly?"

"I'm a research scientist in a biotech lab. I get to analyze the genomes from a variety of organisms and determine if a particular DNA sequence can be used in a more creative way—like getting a cancer cell to cannibalize itself so the cancer goes away, or manipulating viruses into doing something they weren't programmed to do. Not exactly an exciting profession...unless you're a scientist."

The truth was, I found my work to be fascinating, not to mention the research was important. Every discovery was a step closer to helping to cure people in the world living with different diseases. My hope was to find ways of suppressing certain diseases, to keep people from getting sick in the first place. But once I started talking about my field of study, I could see my friends' eyes start to glaze over. Which was why I rarely talked about what I was doing to very many people.

"So you're brilliant?" Gavin concluded, bumping his shoulder against mine teasingly.

I watched as our dogs got tired of wrestling with each other and headed to the doggie water fountain before answering, trying not to blush. "I'm not that smart."

"Now you're just outright lying to me, 'cause we both know that's a load of bullshit." He shook his head, teasing me. "I bet most guys are so intimidated by you, they just don't know what to do other than crawl back to where they came from."

"I wouldn't say they're intimidated," I countered. "They're actually...bored."

Hence, the reason I very rarely dated. I had yet to find a man I had much in common with. And if they were smart enough not to be intimidated or bored by me, then there were other issues, like they were jerks, or simply weren't interested.

Yeah, I knew guys weren't *all* like that, but I had yet to meet a boy who checked even some of the boxes, who wasn't already married or involved in a serious relationship. I was pretty much convinced all the good ones were taken, and I was going to be the oldest virgin walking the face of the Earth.

"Well, I'm not the least bit bored," Gavin replied. "I think you're gorgeous. I know you're smart. And you like dogs. Can't say you could be any more perfect, Charlie."

I turned my attention from our dogs back to Gavin, wondering if he was being sarcastic. Before I could ask, I saw the molten heat in his eyes as he looked at me, and it made me jittery in a way I'd never felt before.

Part lust.

Part fear.

Part longing.

I swallowed hard to rid myself of the ginormous lump in my throat before I said, "I'm not attractive. I'm pretty much invisible to everyone except my friends and family."

"Then everyone else must be blind. But I'll tell you what..." he said in a husky voice. "I can see you clear as day, and I stand by what I said."

Evidently, he did, if the determination in his voice was anything to go by. Maybe that was why he made me so nervous. He pretty much knew nothing about me, but yet the way he looked at me suggested he thought I really *was* attractive.

He's the first guy who doesn't make me feel like I don't measure up to his standards.

I didn't need a therapist to tell me that most of my feelings of inadequacy came from my father. I'd spent most of my life feeling like I was nothing more than a nuisance to my father... that I didn't measure up.

He'd always wanted a boy—but he got me. And then when he finally got the son he'd been dreaming of, tragedy stole him away just seven years later—and I lived with that guilt every day. My mom then died of cancer two years later, though truth be told, she too had been withdrawn after my brother's death.

I'd spent my entire life trying to make my parents happy, yet it hadn't mattered how many academic awards I'd gotten, or how much I accomplished. My mother remained consumed by her grief, and my father would never accept the fact that I lived that tragic day, and my little brother died. My presence only served to remind him of that, every time he laid eyes on me—and he'd never let me forget that.

"I think Thor wants his ball." I nodded at Gavin's furry friend who was waiting not-so-patiently beside his master, relieved to have a distraction from my thoughts, even if my sadness was harder to shake. Yet, I managed a smile, not wanting to ruin what was turning out to be a great day.

The beast was wiggling with excitement, obviously waiting for Gavin to do something. Since the canine's eyes seemed fixated on the ball beside his owner's thigh, I was assuming he wanted Gavin to toss it. I found it funny that Ripley seemed to be just as excited as Thor, even though she wasn't really a fetcher. My girl was just feeding off Thor's excitement.

Gavin let the ball fly with a powerful throw that had the two dogs scrambling after it, although I'd have to say that Ripley was just more or less following Thor's lead.

"I think my girl is in love," I said with a sigh as I watched Ripley start to tussle with Thor over the ball.

"Thor is fixed." Gavin shook his head with a laugh. "I'm just mentioning it because I guarantee that he'll eventually try to hump her and I don't want you worrying about it."

I snorted. "Ripley is fixed, too. And that's why I got a female. I hate the whole humping-the-leg thing. It's so annoying."

Gavin started coughing hard, and I wasn't sure whether he was choking or laughing.

"Are you okay?" I asked, concerned.

He held up a hand. "Yep. I'm fine."

Gavin seemed recovered, so I assumed he was just coughing. "You sure?"

He nodded. "Do you always just blurt out anything that comes into your head?"

I thought about his question for a moment before I replied. "Not always. But I didn't think you'd mind. Did I say something wrong?"

He grinned at me. "Not at all. I like it. I don't exactly get a lot of conversation in my line of work. It's nice to have somebody to talk to who doesn't have a problem saying exactly what they're thinking."

"I can relate to that predicament," I mused. "I don't have much family around here, and all my friends are busy with work and starting families."

He didn't look at me. Gavin seemed focused on a guy across the park who was casually leaning against a tree.

Finally, he asked, "Your job must keep you pretty isolated, huh?"

I shrugged. "Pretty much. I spend a lot of time in protective gear running tests and studying samples. There's generally not a lot of conversation at work, and if we do talk, it's about our project."

"Your project... what exactly are you working on?" Gavin asked as he continued to eye the man across the park from us.

His question caught me a bit off guard. No one had ever wanted to know any of the details when it came to my work. Maybe it was his way of showing me he was interested. "It always changes, depending on the project we're on, but at the moment, I'm developing vaccines for potentially deadly viruses."

"Nothing secret?"

"No. Not really. Why?" Okay... maybe this was getting just a bit odd.

His blue eyes locked on mine. "Charlie, I know you really don't know me. But I need you to do something for me. Okay?"

I frowned at him, just noticing that the guy Gavin was watching was slowly moving closer to us.

"Do you have a leash for Ripley?"

"Yes." It was hanging from the back pocket on my jeans. I was literally sitting on it.

"Call her and put on her leash."

"Why?"

"Please just do it," he rasped.

He called Thor, and the two pups raced back to us together. Gavin was quick to pull a short leash from inside his jacket and clip it to his pup's collar. I did the same with Ripley just on instinct.

I had no idea what was wrong with Gavin, but he'd suddenly become deadly serious. It prompted me to do what he told me to do.

He stood and held out his hand, and I didn't hesitate to grasp it as I got up. "Gavin, what's wrong?"

"Walk with me," he insisted.

His pace was brutally fast, his long legs eating up so much ground as he moved forward that I was trotting next to him with Ripley in tow.

We went through the gate of the park, and walked directly to a vehicle parked on a side street. Gavin pulled out a set of

keys and with a click of a button, he was opening the cargo area
of a luxury SUV. Thor took the jump into the vehicle easily, but
Ripley hesitated. Without missing a beat, Gavin picked her up and
placed her with Thor in the back, then lowered the cargo door.

"I'm sorry to scare you like this, but we need to go," he said
urgently.

"I can't just leave with you," I argued. That would be *insane*.

"You have to, Charlie. I don't have time to explain, but I swear
on Thor's life, you're in danger. Your life depends on it," Gavin
answered huskily. "*Please*. I'll explain as soon as we're out of here
and you're safe."

I'd been a city girl most of my life, and I knew better than to
hop into a vehicle with a man I didn't know. But my gut instinct
told me I could trust Gavin, and with his words sending a shiver of
fear down my spine, I hopped into the car the minute he opened
the passenger door, hoping I hadn't just made a huge mistake.

"Seatbelt," Gavin insisted as he got in behind the wheel,
started the SUV and shot out into traffic. "And I need you to
pull the battery out of your phone."

"Are you going to tell me what's going on?" I asked breathlessly as I buckled myself in, and started fiddling around with
my cell battery.

"Shortly," he answered abruptly, his focus on driving and
checking out the surrounding area.

"For God's sake, Gavin. Tell me what the hell is going on.
You're scaring me."

"That's the last thing I want to do," he replied remorsefully.
"I'm truly sorry. I was hoping I'd have time for you to learn to
trust me before this all went to hell."

I rolled my eyes. "Obviously I *do* trust you or I wouldn't be
in your car with my dog."

"Yeah. That's a very bad idea by the way," he chastised with
a hint of one of his smiles, which eased the knot in my gut just
a little.

"You're stalling," I told him.

"Maybe. But that's because there's no easy way to tell you this." He entered the freeway and gunned the engine.

I growled in frustration. *"Tell me what?"*

"That somebody wants you dead."

CHAPTER 3

Gavin

ell, fuck! This hasn't exactly gone as planned.

Problem was, I just didn't have the time or the luxury of getting to know Charlie before I told her the truth about why I'd been looking for her. Honestly, I couldn't even believe she'd gotten into the vehicle with me. Damn! That could be dangerous.

Mental note: Teach Charlie not to get into vehicles with strange men.

I was both pissed off and relieved that she was sitting here beside me. And I wasn't quite sure how to rationally deal with the two entirely different emotions at one time.

The asshole who'd been watching Charlie didn't appear to be following us. When we'd gone out the gate of the dog park, he'd still been a fair distance away. And we didn't have a tail.

I didn't think it was a coincidence that the guy hadn't taken his eyes away from Charlie, but maybe I'd jumped the gun just little. Though better safe than sorry. Right now, I was suspicious of *anybody* who was watching her that closely.

"I-I don't understand," she said awkwardly.

She sounded terrified now, and my heart sank. She was so sweet, so adorable that the last thing I wanted to do was upset her. But hell, she needed protection right now, and I wasn't going to take any chances. I had no idea why somebody wanted her dead, but until I figured it out, she needed to stay away from any place she normally frequented. Nobody knew me. I wasn't associated with her in any way.

If anybody could hide her, it was me.

"Please don't be afraid. Not of me," I said in a milder tone. "I'm here to help you. I didn't search you out to hurt you. I was just worried someone would get to you before I could warn you."

"You were looking for me? Us meeting up wasn't an accident?"

Smart woman! "I was looking for you because somebody put a paid hit out on you, Charlie. I don't why, and I don't know when it will happen. But I'm worried that you're already under surveillance. That man at the park... I didn't like the way he was looking at you."

"That's crazy," she answered, sounding confused. "I don't have any enemies. I'm a scientist. Why would anybody want to murder me?"

"I wish I knew the answer to that question." Even though I didn't detect anyone following us, I still weaved in and out of traffic on the way to my house, keeping an eye out for anybody tailing me.

"There's nobody after me," she answered with certainty.

"No old, pissed-off boyfriends?" I wasn't sure I wanted to hear her answer.

"None," she answered immediately. "I haven't had a date in years."

Damn! I didn't want to admit to myself how glad I was to hear *that.* "Work? Anybody there?"

She let out an exasperated sigh, but it took her a few moments to answer. "No. I don't think anybody there wants me dead."

Her hesitation to answer caught my attention. "Something happened. What?"

"Nothing worth killing somebody over," she said hastily.

"Tell me."

"I found out something strange a day or two ago. That's all."

"What?" I prompted.

"I'm involved with a research team, right now we're working on a vaccine for a potentially deadly virus. When I finished some of my research, I gave it to my boss Thursday night. I picked it up from him yesterday morning so I could keep adding to my notes, but along with my work was an additional folder with some other research inside it, as if he'd grabbed both by accident or they'd stuck together or something. It appeared to be studies and tests on a deadly virus to see how it can be replicated and grown rather than looking for a vaccine. And from what I could tell, it was level four biohazard rated—the worst of the worst. We don't deal with viruses at level four. There are only a small number of labs that can."

"What did you do when you found out the information wasn't yours?"

"I took it into my boss, Doug Whitman. Explained that he'd accidentally given me another file. But when I asked him about the level four virus and where it was being tested, he looked sort of freaked out, though he tried to hide it. He snagged the file from me, and made up some excuse. Said it wasn't anything we were working on at our lab, but a friend's research that he was reviewing, since that the information was sensitive and I couldn't share any of the details with anyone."

"Did he say anything else about the file?"

"No. Other than his warning to not tell, he didn't want to talk about it—said it was his friend's research and none of our concern. I tried to tell him that I was worried. The virus is deadly. And according to the data in that file, it looked to me like somebody was trying to find a way to spread it instead of eradicating it. Something like that could kill off millions of people. I tried to make my boss realize just how dangerous it could be if it got released, but he just told me it was nothing to worry about, and not to share the information because it was just a simulation of what *could* happen."

"Did you believe that?"

She shrugged. "I don't know. I mean, why would anybody need that sort of data if they weren't thinking of using it in that way, though... I suppose it could be that they were trying to find a way to counter it. But... I don't know. It didn't feel that way."

Everything was pointing in that direction. "So this virus... you think it could be used as some kind of biological warfare?"

Shit! It was a horrifying thought, but what if Charlie had accidentally interfered with a study on biological warfare? The money to be made from selling off information like that to other countries was astronomical. However, most of the countries who would want that type of thing were *not* our allies. That was probably the scariest part.

"Honestly, yes. The methods of replication and some of the other information looked exactly like it was being designed to be used as a weapon. I know it's not logical—"

"It is logical in an insane type of way, Charlie. Think about it. Biological weapons are highly sought out in some countries, and the payment would be enough to make somebody incredibly rich. Someone could use the virus to manufacture a dirty bomb, which is a hell of a lot more difficult to detect."

"But, we're scientists. We use our knowledge to do good things," she answered, sounding confused.

I shook my head, just a little bit enchanted by how naïve Charlie was when it came to being bad. "Money, or even the possibility of being filthy rich changes people."

I didn't want to tell her that some people were just inherently evil. I was certain she knew those people existed, but I wasn't sure she'd even encountered them up close and personal.

I'd seen enough cold-blooded murderers in prison to make my skin crawl, bastards who would slit somebody's throat and wallow in the blood without a hint of remorse.

"Okay," she finally answered. "But that still doesn't explain why anyone would be after *me*. Even if somebody at the lab is working with deadly viruses to try to make a biological weapon, I'm certainly not the one doing it."

"If what you saw was their research to make those weapons, you're a threat to the whole organization. I guarantee it goes a hell of a lot higher than just your boss, and there has to be more people involved in this crime. Something worth that much money is worth killing for in some people's mind. Keeping it a secret is essential. They can't risk having you go to the authorities. It's likely why they put a hit on you. I'm just glad I came across it on the dark web."

"You found the hit on the dark web? Why were you there?"

I was relieved that she didn't sound accusatory. She just sounded...confused. Not that I blamed her. Just taking in the fact that somebody might want her dead was probably a lot to handle. Hell, I was used to it. I'd made a lot of enemies. But Charlie was just doing her job. I vaguely wondered if she'd ever even gotten a parking ticket.

I answered as I got off the freeway. "You can call it a hobby, I guess. One of my personal missions is to hack the dark web, and try to find a way to obliterate it from the internet completely. It's a nest for pedophiles, murderers, sex trafficking, and a lot of other things we could do without in this world. So I spend my free time hacking into the information available and trying to block it or dismantle some of the operations there."

She shuddered. "So that's where you ran into the hit on me?"

"Yeah. I'm sorry that I had to tell you about it so soon. I was hoping I could get you to trust me, instead of freaking you out like this. But I don't know that we have the luxury of time. It's Saturday. The hit was placed last night, and it wouldn't have taken long for somebody to find you once someone took the job. You weren't exactly hiding."

"I didn't know somebody wanted me dead," she replied in a forlorn tone.

"I'll keep you safe, Charlie. I promise."

"Where are we going?"

"My place. You and I have no previous association, and I have a damn good security system. We'll figure things out from there. Right now, all I want is to keep you safe."

"I still can't fathom that all this is true, but if it is...thank you."

"For what?"

"You may be saving my life."

I didn't bother to explain it might get a whole lot worse before it got better. "I have some government contacts. I'll call them when we get to my house."

"What if it's a false alarm, or a misunderstanding?"

"I'm damn good at what I do, Charlie." I was skilled enough to land myself in prison for doing it, but I wasn't about to tell her that at the moment. "There *is* a hit out on you. It's not an error. I want to call in the FBI and a couple of friends to help."

"I'll tell them anything I can." She let out a ragged breath, as if she'd been holding it. "In some ways, I'm actually relieved."

"Because you have somebody out there who wants you dead?" I asked in a bewildered voice.

"No. I'm glad that at least the information I saw is going to be investigated. I'm generally not the type to panic, but I wasn't really buying what my boss told me. I guess it's possible that somebody was just messing around, but they'd need the virus to study in order to get the results I was seeing. And Doug, my boss, seemed really nervous. I've been thinking about this whole situation since he took the file back from me yesterday."

"Gut instinct?" I suggested.

"Yeah. Not to mention the detailed report. It was *not* good, Gavin."

"You were already thinking about talking to somebody, weren't you," I guessed.

"Yeah... I just wasn't sure where to go. If it was nothing, I knew I'd lose my job, but I was willing to take the risk."

I nodded. "That's why they want you dead."

"The pieces all make sense, I guess. But is money really worth killing somebody?"

"You'd be surprised how many sick people are out there who think it is. But being rich only feels good to me when I've actually earned it honestly."

She turned her head to look at me. "Does that mean you're wealthy?"

I tossed her a smile. "Just a little, though I'll admit, I'm pretty damn proud of what I've managed to accomplish. Me and my partner, Kane... we've worked our asses off for every damn penny we earned." I took pride in my success now. But there was a time when I'd hated myself for the things I'd done.

I turned into the driveway of my Medina waterfront home and stopped at the gate to enter the code.

"Holy crap! You live *here*?" Charlie's voice was filled with excitement.

"I love this place," I answered as I navigated through the gate and up the winding drive.

"Who wouldn't?"

There had been a time when I couldn't have even afforded the bus fare to get to this obscenely rich neighborhood. Remembering those times kept me grounded. "I've been lucky. I have a good partner. And our business is lucrative."

"I'm sure you've worked hard," she argued. "Nobody does that well without a little luck and a lot of ambition."

I shrugged, almost embarrassed by her praise. I really didn't deserve it. I'd gone to prison and done some horrible things in my past. Anything good I was doing now was never going to change my past.

I took her and the dogs inside after parking my vehicle in one of several garages. When we entered the kitchen, I asked, "Are you hungry?"

"Honestly, no. Finding out somebody might be trying to kill me kind of ruined my appetite."

I put my hands on her shoulders. When she looked up at me with her expressive dark eyes, I nearly lost it. "Charlie, I won't let anything happen to you. We'll find out who set this up and why."

"What do I do now? Do I go to work and pretend like nothing ever happened? Do I resign? My work is my life, Gavin."

"I know how hard this must be for you." I spent most of my time in front of a computer, obsessed with my job, and my personal pursuits to end as much of the bullshit as possible on the dark web. "But you can't go to work. You can't call them. Give me some time. Please."

Hell, I was desperate to put her mind at ease, but there was no way in hell she could get near that lab until we knew who put the hit out on her.

"Right now, I just want to go back to my boring life," she said in a voice so sad that I couldn't help but wrap my arms around her and hold her tightly in my grasp.

Her arms crept slowly around my waist, and even though she didn't cry, I could feel her body trembling with fear. "Don't be scared, Charlie. I know this is all really weird, but we'll figure it out."

I cursed my unruly dick as it sprang to life the moment I felt her body against me, inhaled her scent, and felt her warm breath against my neck. Fuck... The sensations were intoxicating as hell.

I was disappointed when she drew away to look at me. "Why are you doing this, Gavin? Why get involved in a situation that has nothing to do with you."

"Because it's the right thing to do." I knew I was being vague, but I didn't want to explain how I'd learned the hard way about right and wrong.

"I guess I'm crashing at your place for a while," she said with a nervous smile.

Charlie could move in permanently, and I doubted that I'd ever regret it. She affected me *just that much.* It wasn't comfortable, and feeling this way wasn't something I wanted, but damned if I could stop myself from wishing I could get this woman into my bed.

But it was more than that.

I actually…liked her. She was beautiful, smart, funny, and definitely kind to animals. It wasn't a lot to go on to explain my attraction to her. I'd met plenty of beautiful women. But this one was different. I felt like we understood one another, and I'd never experienced that before.

I shrugged. "Make yourself at home. I'll start making some calls."

I let go of her completely so I could go to my office and start phoning some of my contacts. I wanted to start looking around the dark net for any other clues about who was after Charlie.

"Gavin?" Her voice was hesitant as I started toward my office.

I turned back toward her. "Yeah?"

She didn't speak. Confusion, fear, anger and several other emotions flashed in her eyes, and she opened her mouth and then closed it again.

I moved closer to her again. "Are you okay?"

She shook her head, making her braids bounce around on her shoulders. "I don't think I am. This all seems so surreal. Maybe I'm just feeling…lost."

I cursed myself for not handling all of this a little bit smoother. This was a woman who had never lived in my world, a woman who'd been educated and had probably never come close to a bad neighborhood, or a prison for that matter.

I held out my hand. "Would it help if you stayed with me?"

She seemed to consider my words for a moment and then nodded. "I think it would. I just don't want to be alone."

The fact that she was starting to trust me made my chest ache. "Come on. We'll do this together. If two geeks can't figure it out together, I'm not sure who can."

Just like I'd hoped, she smiled, then placed her hand in mine. "I'm the science geek," she answered.

"I've been a misfit most of my life," I told her openly, honestly. It was the truth. I'd never quite fit in, and very few people understood me. I was different, the type of person who was just fine in my own little world.

"Me, too," she confessed.

Maybe I'd never realized how lonely I'd always been.

Or there was a chance that Charlie was a kindred spirit.

Whatever it was, it felt good to have her here. And I was damn happy that thinking about something from the dark web had kept me up all night until I figured out the mystery.

If I hadn't, there was every possibility that this adorable, smart female might already be dead.

I had to struggle with my anger at the thought of anyone harming Charlie as I threaded my fingers through hers and dragged her toward my office.

CHAPTER 4

Charlie

I couldn't get my thoughts to slow as I curled up on the lounger in Gavin's office and attempted to read a book I'd grabbed from his massive library. How the hell did I, of all people, end up with a hit out on my life? Everything I did was as risk-free as one could get. I didn't take chances or put myself in danger, and I sure as hell didn't ever put my life on the line.

My one brush with death had been more than enough for me, teaching me a lesson early in life, when I was just ten years old. And it was one hell of a lesson to learn. I knew how lucky I was to still be alive—especially when my seven-year-old brother didn't survive that tragic day. I was here, but he wasn't, his precious life cut short.

I'd wished a million times over to trade places with Jessie, to have it be him who got pulled from the freezing water and cracked ice instead of me, to have his life be spared instead of mine. But those weren't the cards fate dealt us that day. *No...* I was the one who got to live another day and my brother didn't—something my father never failed to remind me of.

"Hey… you okay?" Gavin swiveled away from the multiple monitors that lined his desk, and reached over to run a comforting hand down my arm.

"Yeah… no… sorry, I guess I'm not. I just can't believe that this is actually happening to me. I swear, I don't think my boss knows the first thing about hiring a hitman." It's not that he wasn't a big enough asshole to develop a viral weapon if it meant lining his pockets. But putting a hit out on me felt like such an extreme, especially when I'd done nothing more than stumble across the data and bring it to his attention. "Honestly, I didn't even quite realize what I'd come across when I first found the data on those viral specimens. I thought it was just a dangerous mistake—until I took a closer look. But… this just all seems surreal."

"I know I've only just met you, but I suspect you always see the best in people. And if you do everything by the book, you probably think everyone else does too. But there's no point in worrying about this when we're already doing all we can to keep you safe." Gavin got to his feet, stretching out his massive form, and then offered me his hand. "Come on, sweetness… I'm starving, and I work better when I keep myself fed. Besides… you should really eat something. There's nothing like low blood sugar levels to make everything seem a million times worse."

Setting the book aside, I let him pull me up out of the chaise, though having him so close only served to remind me that I hadn't been on an actual date in so long that I'd actually need both hands to count the years. "I can cook if you want. I'm not half bad."

Our two pups got to their feet the moment they realized food was being discussed. Gavin smiled, shaking his head. "I see Ripley has food ESP too. I swear, if I so much as think of food or a walk, Thor immediately picks up on it without me ever speaking a word or moving a muscle."

"It's crazy, isn't it?" Though what was crazier was the fact that I had a hit out on my life and I was flirting with the most gorgeous man I'd ever laid eyes on.

Not that I was flirting.

Because flirting when someone was trying to kill you just did *not* make sense. Nor did trusting someone I'd only just met. Yet here I was, even though I could hear my father's voice telling me that I was nothing but a useless fool to trust someone I didn't know.

I pushed away all thoughts of my father, not wanting to start doubting myself. Following behind Gavin, he led the way towards his kitchen, which gave me the chance to see more of his amazing home. It was the perfect blend of casual masculinity with touches that made it uniquely his, with sci-fi collectibles gracing the walls and shelves throughout the home. Clearly, he wasn't someone who was out to impress, but rather had put together a home that was truly his.

That said, the kitchen we walked into would've impressed even the top chefs of the world. "Holy smokes. Tell me you actually use this kitchen, and it's not just for show."

"I cook a fair bit, though to be honest, it's more out of necessity rather than passion. I tend to keep the local take-out joints plenty busy, but that doesn't really work for the five meals I eat a day, not to mention the three am binges that happen when I'm working late—which is all the time." Gavin pulled open the fridge door, and poked around. "Not sure what you're in the mood for. I've got a few steaks I could grill. It'd give the dogs a chance to run around a bit before settling in for the night."

"Steaks are great." I loved how he didn't just think of me, but also the dogs. Yet given that someone might be out to kill me, I wasn't sure how careful I needed to be. The last thing I wanted to do is get taken out by some sniper. "And... it'll be safe for me to be outside?"

"My property is well secured, and at the moment, no one knows you're with me. There's nothing connecting the two of us. And with luck, your boss hasn't noticed that I took down his job for a hitman. Until he puts another one back up, you're safe." Gavin grabbed everything he'd need to cook us dinner and led the way out onto the back deck, off the kitchen, the dogs zipping past us to run around. "Make yourself at home. These shouldn't take long to cook."

"Anything I can do to help?" This all felt so surreal as I stood there by his side.

Not only did I not know him, but this was a completely unfamiliar environment, and I was simply handing my life over to him. Sure, he was funny, and he seemed really nice, but I didn't exactly have a whole lot of experience when it came to men, or even being street-smart. My father always said I was too naïve for my own good. And maybe he was right.

Yet as I looked over at Gavin, nothing about him set off any warning bells—other than the fact that he was a complete stranger. And though there'd been no visible threat, he had still whisked me away in his vehicle and into his home. I didn't know the first thing about him, and yet I was essentially putting my life in his hands.

Maybe I just needed to get to know him better. Then I wouldn't feel as naïve and trusting, and maybe my dad's voice rattling around in my head would just shut the hell up. Not that it ever did. He'd never been happy with anything I'd managed to accomplish, no matter how hard I'd tried. Never a kind word, or a show of affection. Nothing was ever good enough. Because I wasn't his boy—and nothing could bring Jessie back.

Determined to prove my father wrong, even though it was all in my head, I wandered over to Gavin's side, determined to get to know him a bit better so that I'd know for sure that he was just a nice guy and I hadn't been wrong to trust him. "I have to admit, this all feels so bizarre. I don't even remember your last name… And anything other than knowing that you wander about the dark web trying to save clueless scientists from getting their head blown off."

He let out a laugh, tossing me a smile that had my heart pounding double-time. "Last name's Reid—and honestly there isn't much else to know. You already know that I have a tech security company with my best friend, and I'd like to think I'm the top in my field. I grew up dirt poor, so I appreciate the things I now have. I have a younger brother and sister, both of whom work for me, in different capacities. I have no kids, never been married or engaged, and other than work and Thor, my life is pretty uneventful. How about you?"

The last thing I wanted to do is tell him about my messed up family life. That would have to wait. And so I gave him a smile, hoping he wouldn't ask too many questions.

"My life has been pretty boring—up until this morning. I have a feeling that meeting you… it's changed everything."

CHAPTER 5

Gavin

I felt guilty about giving Charlie nothing more than the cursory facts about my life, taking care not to mention anything that might freak her out—like the fact that I'd done a couple stints in prison. Granted it was for hacking, rather than anything violent or more serious, but the time I spent on the inside had certainly changed me—and not for the better.

Behind bars, it was all about surviving to see another day, even if it meant doing things you would never in a million years do under normal circumstances. You made enemies you didn't want, brutal and unconscionable men who changed the very person you were... changed the very fabric of your being.

I had secrets—and those secrets came with a lifetime of guilt for the things I'd been forced to do, even if I had no control over what happened. Because there was no changing what was already done, and that meant the guilt was mine to bear.

I shook my head free of my thoughts and turned my focus back to Charlie as we finished eating dinner, having opted to dine indoors, given that the temperature had dropped as the sun set.

"I'm stuffed. That was really good, Gavin." She put her fork down and sat back in her chair. "Um… I don't mean to be a pain, but… I don't have any of my stuff here. And… I can't just stay here indefinitely, though I really do appreciate you going out of your way to help me out. At some point, I'm going to have to head home."

"I'll buy you a new wardrobe first thing in the morning. New laptop, new dog bed… whatever you need. It's not safe for you to go home. Even though I eliminated the hit on your life, I can't guarantee that your boss didn't go another route, and that's not a risk I'm willing to take when it's your life that's on the line." I didn't want to freak her out, but there was no way in hell I was going to let her take unnecessary risks.

"I guess I'm still having a hard time wrapping my head around this new reality." Her brow furrowed with worry as she seemed to mull things over.

"I know you've never had to deal with anything like this before, and it's a drastic change, but we need to be careful, since anyone coming after you will be a professional. Even if I was the one to go to your home, that would then link the two of us, and if your house was being watched, I'd end up leading them right back here." Money wasn't an object, and I'd happily buy her whatever she wanted if it meant keeping her safe. "But I swear, we'll get this sorted out. You have my word. This is all just temporary."

"So, until then, I'm supposed to just stay here and hope that some professional killer doesn't track me down?" Her eyes widened with panic as her new circumstances seemed to settle in.

I reached across the table and gave her hand a squeeze, unable to resist the urge to touch her and ease her concerns. "I'll do all I can to get this taken care of quickly—and I get that this is hard on you. But for now, my priority is keeping you safe."

"I really do appreciate it. But this has been overwhelming— and completely unexpected. I was just doing my job, and now someone wants me dead." She was clearly starting to freak out a little, as her new reality set in. "What if it doesn't stop with just my boss? What if this doesn't stop until I'm dead?"

Unfortunately, she was right. Because her boss was likely working for someone else—most likely the person he was developing the virus for—and people like that didn't like loose ends. And at the moment, that's exactly what Charlie was.

The thought of her coming to harm filled me with a fierce protectiveness, unlike anything I'd felt before, even though I'd only just met her. I couldn't let anything happen to her.

"We'll take every single one of them down. I already sent emails to my connections in the FBI, and I can guarantee you that weaponized viruses aren't something that they're going to take lightly." I didn't know who was involved, or what their motives were, but this sort of thing was a big deal because it could easily involve the deaths of thousands of people.

She nodded, and though she still looked uncertain, she was still handling it better than most would, especially when it all went down in such a hurry, forcing her to trust a complete stranger. "I don't even know what I'd do if it weren't for your help."

"Whatever you need, sweetheart... I'm here for you." My cock went hard as I misconstrued my own words. What the fuck was I thinking? Except that my cock had had a mind all its own from the moment I first laid eyes on her. "I'm not sure what time you normally head to bed, but let me show you to your room so that you can get settled in. I can lend you a T-shirt and sweats, and then you have my word, we'll go shopping first thing in the morning."

I put the dishes in the sink, and then took her by the hand and led her to the nicest of my guestrooms, Thor and Ripley following after us.

In all reality, it was a second master suite, with its own luxurious bath, gorgeous views of the ocean just beyond, and a beautiful and inviting stone fireplace that reached up to the cathedral ceilings, while thick wooden beams crisscrossed overhead.

This house was far larger than I needed it to be, considering how much of a loner I was. But it was great for when family came to visit, or during the holidays when everyone would gather together. And since money wasn't an object at this point in my life, and I had no other expenses, I figured I might as well make this my dream home, especially when I spent most of my time here, since I worked from home. "Here you go. You should have everything you need, other than a change of clothes."

I loved the astounded look in her amber eyes as she took in the room. "Wow... I don't even know what to say, other than this place is amazing."

"I'm glad you like it. There's a nice soaking tub in the bathroom if you want to relax a bit, and a washer and dryer here in the hall if you want to toss your clothes in." After the day she'd had, getting her to unwind a bit may not be a bad idea, though the thought of her naked as she gingerly slipped into steaming hot water had my hard cock aching and straining against the zipper of my jeans. And when I spoke, it was nearly impossible to keep the need from my voice, which was now thick and gruff. "Let me grab those clothes for you."

I headed to my closet and quickly dug around, though anything I had would be swimming on her. Oh well... it'd have to do. I grabbed a T-shirt, hoodie, and a pair of sweats that had a drawstring so she could adjust them, and then headed back to her. "Here you go. I'll be in my office if you need me—but feel free to wander. I want you to feel at home."

Yet before I could go, she grabbed my hand and pulled me to her, looking suddenly shy. "I know I've already said this a million times today, but I can't thank you enough for taking care of me."

And then she went up onto the tips of her toes, and kissed my cheek as her lush curves pressed up against my body, my arms wrapping around her waist to hold her close. Fuck... It was going to be damn hard to let her take the lead and not ravish her. "Charlie..."

There was no hiding just how much I wanted her, but before I could take things any further, she was stepping out of my arms and putting some distance between us, a blush creeping across her cheeks. "I think I'm going to take that bath. Goodnight, Gavin."

"Sweet dreams, love." I forced myself to walk away from her, taken aback by the effect she was having on me.

Even though I didn't date a whole lot, I still went out with my friends, and there was never any shortage of women who were happy to flirt with me and show me they were interested. And though they were usually nice people, and more often than not, gorgeous, I was never drawn to any of them.

But Charlie? The way she made me feel was completely different to anything I'd ever experienced with anyone else. Maybe it was because she was a bit shy, and didn't really see just how beautiful she was. And maybe it was because she was the perfect blend of geeky scientist and sexy girl next door. Basically, she was all a man could ever want—all *I* could ever want.

And it didn't matter one bit that it was insane for me to be having any of these thoughts when I'd only just met her.

All I have to do is keep her safe.

I sat back down in front of my multiple computer screens once I'd arrived back in my office and got to work.

Fuck... The ad had gotten reposted. I took it down again, but I knew that it was only a matter of time before he found another way to hire a hitman or the ad found a taker before I had a chance to take it down. We were safe here, but it might not be a bad idea to get out of town for a bit. Going overseas wasn't an option unless I got her a passport under an alias, but this was a big enough country to get lost in, and I had the means to make it easy.

No matter what, I'd do whatever it took to keep her safe and see her through a situation that had to be like a nightmare scenario for her. I had to. Any other option wasn't acceptable.

CHAPTER 6

Charlie

Despite everything that was going on in my life, I'd managed to sleep remarkably well after the long bath I'd taken. Knowing the dogs had to go out first thing in the morning, I slipped on the clothes Gavin gave me, and though they were far too large, the fabric was soft and smelled like him. I wrapped my arms around myself and breathed in his scent, before padding barefoot out into the living area with Ripley following behind me. I wondered if Gavin was awake yet.

It felt odd wandering through someone else's home, especially when I didn't really know him. He'd said to make myself feel at home, but it still felt odd to be walking through unfamiliar surroundings all on my own. He'd been too busy yesterday to give me the full tour, but I may have to ask for one today. The house was so large that I was likely to get lost if I didn't know the layout.

I quickly let out Ripley and Thor, knowing the yard was fenced, and then continued my search for Gavin.

It wasn't a huge surprise when I found him in his office, and it left me wondering if he'd actually gone to bed last night or if he'd been working this whole time. "Good morning. Please tell me you got to bed at some point last night."

"I got a few hours, but... I don't tend to need much sleep." The light in his eyes darkened just a little, and his smile slipped, though only for a moment. It left me wondering if there was more to it than being an insomniac, though I imagined he was also a pretty busy guy, especially if he had his own company to run, in addition to his side projects. "Are you hungry? I was thinking we could head out and grab a bite before going shopping."

"That sounds perfect, since I could do with more clothes." I had clothes for today, since I'd washed what I had on yesterday when this whole nightmare started, but beyond washing and wearing the same things, day in and day out, I had few other options. "Will it be okay for me to leave Ripley here while we're gone?"

"I'm sure they'll be fine. And we won't be too long." He got to his feet and crossed to -my side, towering over me and making me feel small, though his smile had returned, making my heart skitter out of control, especially when he ran a gentle hand down my arm. "You should be safe for the next few hours, since I took down the new hit your boss posted. But I've also reached out to my connections in the FBI, and there's still no connection between us, so I don't want you worrying."

"He already put up another hit?" My new reality slammed into me like a runaway freight train. Someone—my boss, presumably—really wanted me dead. And then it hit me. "Gavin... I don't have any evidence on that weaponized virus. I handed it over to my boss, not realizing that he was the one behind it. What if he's already destroyed it?"

Gavin gave me a sexy frown, looking as though he was mulling things over. "If he was the one to take the hit out on you, then they'd still have him for attempted murder, though that would carry a lesser sentence to what would amount as terrorism, or aiding a terrorist or foreign government, depending on who he's working for. If he's hiring a hitman, then it's likely he doesn't want his bosses to know that he basically screwed up. There may be a way for us to use that to our advantage."

It was sounding more and more like getting the FBI involved would be inevitable—which was fine by me. I couldn't deal with the fact that I was a walking target, and even worse was knowing that I might be putting other people at risk, like Gavin. I already had to live with the guilt of my brother's death, and it'd ruin me to have someone else get hurt because of me.

"What if I went into work? It's Sunday, and we'll be running on a limited staff. Though I wouldn't be able to get my hands on the specimens, I still have some of the data at my desk. That might be enough to allow the FBI to get a warrant, so they can lock him up on the greater charges." I was willing to take the risk if it meant no one else got hurt, and the virus stayed out of our enemy's hands.

Gavin's brow furrowed as he looked at me with darkening eyes, shaking his head as he gripped my arms. "No. There's no fucking way I'm letting you go back there when your boss wants you dead. That's not happening, so get it out of your head. You're not going anywhere near the lab or your boss, until he's behind bars."

"But once the FBI has the evidence to lock up my boss, this will be over—and the faster I get the evidence, the better. Don't you think?" That way I could get back to my life. Though it was damn nice to have Gavin around. Having a hit out on my life was more than a little stressful and a whole lot scary.

"Not if the people your boss is working for decide they want to tie up loose ends and eliminate any witnesses." He shook his head as I tried to fight back the panic that was running through my veins like ice. "I'm sorry, Charlie, but you just need to trust me on this one. And I get it—you don't know me, so why should you do anything I say. But I swear, I'm just trying to keep you safe."

"I know." It didn't matter that I barely knew Gavin. For whatever reason, I trusted him, and until he gave me a reason not to, I'd likely listen to what he had to say. "It's just that yesterday morning, my life was still completely normal. And now... It's just a lot to take in and adjust to."

"I know it is, love." When he pulled me into the protective comfort of his strong arms, it felt all too natural to be there.

I held onto him, resting my head against his muscular chest as he engulfed me in his embrace and I breathed in his clean, masculine scent. There in his arms, everything felt so right, even if my life was in complete turmoil. It was almost as if fate was trying to bring us together.

Except that there was a reason why I'd been single most of my life—a reason why I was still a virgin. I had no self-confidence in anything but my work, and if my father was to be believed, I didn't deserve to be happy. Not when my life had been chosen over my little brother's.

Yet I couldn't do anything but hold onto Gavin, as if he was the lifeline I'd been waiting for all along. And when he tightened his hold on me and pressed his scruffy cheek to the top of my head, it somehow felt as if, for just that moment, I'd been absolved of all my sins.

We stayed that way, locked together, for what felt like an eternity, as if all of time stood still in that moment. And though Gavin didn't let go of me, he did pull away just enough to look at me, his blue eyes taking me in. He brushed my hair from my eyes and cupped my cheek, his touch lingering as I resisted the urge to lean in and kiss him. "You have me worried about you, Charlie."

"I've got you watching my back, right? That means everything will be okay."

CHAPTER 7

Gavin

The way Charlie looked at me, like I was her knight in shining armor... it just reminded me that my life was messed up. And given my past, she definitely deserved better.

I wasn't *anyone's* knight, and it didn't matter that I wanted to kiss her, nor did it matter that I wanted to scoop her up off her feet and carry her off to my bed to ravage her. And so, despite the insatiable need to kiss her, I let go of her and took a step back.

Fuck. I hated the disappointed look in her eyes. But what was the point? She sure as hell wasn't the sort of girl you simply hooked up with for a bit of fun. And that meant she was off limits, even if it was going to be damn hard to keep my distance. "Come on, love. I'm starving, and you have some shopping to do."

She nodded, managing a small smile, though it didn't reach her eyes—and I knew damn well that it was my fault. I wanted nothing more than to kiss her, but this wasn't about my needs—it was about her, and I knew I'd be no good for her when I was still dealing with all my issues.

She must've seen the hesitation in my eyes, because once again her disappointment was clear. She put some distance between us, leaving me to hate myself. "Lead the way."

I swallowed down a low grumble and reached out to take her hand, needing the physical connection between us, even though I'd been pushing her away. "I think it's probably best if we head into the city, just as a precaution. There's this great little diner I know. They make the best chicken and waffles."

She followed me out to my car and we got on the road. "Isn't chicken and waffles a southern thing? You don't get too much of that here in Seattle."

"You're right. It is a southern thing, but it seems like the combination is classic enough to become a popular choice around the country. And this place does a damn good job of it." At least with the conversation going, she seemed to be back to her normal cheery self, her disappointment quickly fading. "So... Tell me a little bit more about yourself."

"Honestly, there isn't much to tell. Other than Ripley and my job... I don't have much of a life. I spend my free time either going for runs with Ripley, reading, or binge watching my favorite shows. Oh!" She grabbed my arm and shifted in her seat to face me, her amber eyes alight. "And I do a bit of crafting too."

Her sudden enthusiasm had me laughing—and I loved that she wasn't letting her current situation drag her down too much. "What kind of crafting?"

"I sew fleece dog coats and comfy blankets for the local shelters, and you're going to think it's silly, but... I make costumes for cosplay events. I know—I couldn't be any more of a geek, huh?" The blush that flushed her cheeks made her look adorable, but I hated that she'd feel embarrassed or uncomfortable about something that she was passionate about.

"I think it's fucking awesome that you've got a creative side to you, in addition to being so into science. And don't even get me started on what you're doing for all those shelter animals." How could she not think those things were amazing? I hated that she questioned herself, and it left me wondering who the hell had messed with her head. "As far as I'm concerned, you're perfect."

Her cheeks turned scarlet as she shook her head no, clearly not used to anyone complimenting her. "Trust me, I'm not."

"I beg to differ, love." But I wouldn't argue with her any further. I'd just need to prove it to her, slowly but surely, until she finally came to terms with how special she was. "Tell me more... where did you grow up? Where did you go to college? How about your family? Any brothers or sisters, or are you an only child?"

I wanted to know everything about her, even as I ignored the voice in my head that told me I was better off keeping my distance, and no good would come from getting attached to her.

"I grew up in Minnesota, north of Minneapolis, but wanted a change of pace so I came out here to Seattle for college. Did my undergrad and graduate work at UW." She bit her bottom lip and looked at the hands in her lap, before continuing. "As for family, it's just me and my dad now, though he's still back in Minnesota."

The pain in her voice broke my heart, and though I was driving, I couldn't help but reach over and pull her against me, kissing the top of her head. I didn't know what had happened, but I thought it telling that she was here in Seattle, even though her dad was on his own halfway across the country. Or maybe he wasn't alone anymore. Maybe he'd remarried... or maybe their relationship was strained. One way or another, it was clearly a topic that carried some emotion with it, and at this point, she had more than enough on her plate to deal with without me opening up old wounds.

"We're nearly there." I turned down the road the restaurant was on, and then parked, once we got close. Jogging around to her side of the vehicle, I pulled open her door, loving the smile she gave me as she let me take her hand and help her down from my SUV. Not that I'd be letting go of her hand now that I had it in mine.

I scanned the area as we walked, wanting to make sure there weren't any threats around, even though, logically, I knew that no one had picked up the hit yet and there was no way of anyone tracking her to our location. Still... I'd feel better once we weren't out in the open.

Luckily, we didn't have more than a ten-minute wait for a table, and before long we were both sitting down to a pile of fried chicken and waffles, drizzled with warm maple syrup that had been doctored to give it just a little bit of spice. "What do you think? It's good, right?"

"It's a hell of a lot better than good, Gavin. This has to be one of the best things I've eaten in a very long time—and that's saying something, given that Seattle is such a foodie city." Her lips glistened with maple syrup as she smiled at me, making it nearly impossible for me to resist leaning in and kissing her.

One thing was for sure... Keeping my distance? That wasn't going to be easy.

CHAPTER 8

Charlie

*G*avin's blue eyes were smoldering with heat as I looked up at him, realizing that I'd been stuffing myself like a woman who hadn't eaten in days. My tongue darted out to lick my lips, realizing they were syrupy sweet with maple syrup.

My dad had always chastised me about my table manners. Yet I pushed thoughts of him and his words from my mind, not wanting Gavin to start asking questions. He noticed everything, that was for sure.

I dropped my food back on my plate and awkwardly reached for a napkin, doing my best to clean up the stickiness on my face. "I'm sorry. My manners are horrible. I'm used to eating alone."

"Hey," Gavin said in a low quiet voice. "Don't ever second-guess yourself with me. I love a woman who enjoys her food. And I'm just as sticky and greasy. But that's what good food is about, right? Simply enjoying it."

It was true that he was enjoying himself, since he'd already devoured most of his meal, and he hadn't had any issue using his hands for the chicken. And his lips were shiny with syrup—just like mine.

45

"You have some…" I pointed to my own face trying to let him know that there was bit of crumb in his stubble, but when he went to the opposite side, I grabbed my napkin and quickly wiped it from his face before I could think about my actions. "All set."

Yet, I suddenly felt ignorant and stupid. What sort of woman cleans up a guy she barely knows? I dropped my hand and my gaze lowered to my plate.

"Hey, love… what's wrong?" Gavin set aside his fork, his gaze focusing on me as if I was the only thing that mattered. "You're not eating."

"I guess I wasn't as hungry as I thought," I answered vaguely.

Gavin reached over and gently tipped my face up to look at him. "Talk to me, Charlie… I hate it when your smile fades to nothing. Tell me what's wrong. Because you seemed to be enjoying yourself just moments earlier, and now…"

"It's nothing." I thought of my father who always told me I ate like a pig.

He shook his head. "It doesn't look like nothing—and I want you to be able to talk to me. About anything. And I can't imagine what's upset you when we were doing nothing but enjoying a damn good meal."

I shrugged. "I guess I'm just a bit self-conscious. My table manners… My dad… he always used to tell me that I didn't eat like a civilized person."

"That's a load of crap, Charlie." Gavin's eyes flared with anger. Yet I couldn't remember if anyone had ever gotten angry on my behalf—and it only endeared him to me all the more. "How exactly would he eat *his* chicken and waffles?"

I nearly laughed at the thought of my father eating in a place like this. "First off, he wouldn't be caught dead eating chicken and waffles. But if by some fluke he had to, I can guarantee you, he'd be cutting his chicken with a knife, and he'd never in a million years use his hands."

A puzzled look appeared on Gavin's face. "Who in the hell uses a knife and fork to eat fried chicken?"

I shifted my attention away from his gaze, unable to handle the intensity of his ocean-blue stare. Sometimes, I swore he could see right through me. "My father."

I'd always been expected to have good manners. Both of my parents had come from wealth, and it seemed like I was forever trying to fit into the world of old money and snobbery.

"Sweetheart, there's something seriously wrong with that," Gavin observed as he picked up a chicken leg and took a bite, as if to make a point.

"You think so?" I asked, slightly bemused as he finished up his chicken, not bothering once with a fork or knife.

"I know so," he said with a knowing smile as he dropped the clean bone on the plate. "Eat, Charlie. There's a good chance you're stuck with me for the foreseeable future, and I'm likely going to offend your sense of etiquette if you never use your hands to eat. Frankly, I'd feel better if you just enjoyed yourself, and ate with me, instead of second guessing everything you do."

A small smile did form on my lips as I picked up a chicken leg. "They were never my rules," I explained. "My dad had...high expectations."

I left it at that, not wanting to mention the fact that my father hated me because I was alive, and Jessie was gone.

Gavin continued to devour his meal, clearly enjoying himself. "Your dad has to be damn proud of you, Charlie. You're trying to change the world for the better with your research." He hesitated before he added, "I'll bet you graduated from college with honors."

"Summa cum laude," I admitted hesitantly.

I'd never gotten any grade that was less than perfect in any of my studies. Not since Jessie had died. Sometimes I thought I was trying to prove to my father that I deserved to be alive. But it didn't matter how much I excelled. In my father's eyes, I'd never be able to live up to what Jessie would have been, and all he'd have accomplished, if he'd gotten the chance to live his life.

Gavin gave me a charming smile as he finished his waffle, and then reached for his coffee. "Always perfect."

I didn't know if he meant me—which I wasn't, despite Gavin's delusions—or the coffee, but with my appetite back, we fell into a comfortable silence as we filled our bellies with food. And it really *was* delicious. I couldn't help but let out an occasional little moan at the crispiness of the chicken and the sweetness of the maple syrup—which was the real deal, and not just caramelized sugar water.

The waitress brought us towelettes, and we used most of them to clean off any stickiness at the end of our meal.

"So what's your final verdict?" Gavin asked, his plate clean except for the discarded chicken bones.

"It was amazing," I answered honestly.

"Once you got over using your hands?" he teased.

"I'm sorry," I said in a quiet voice. "Old habits, I'm afraid. I honestly don't cut my fried chicken with a knife. But I didn't want you to think I was barbaric, either."

"I think I'll be fine unless you start tossing your bones on the floor and start calling a serving wench to bring you another tankard of ale," he joked.

I laughed freely at his joke, almost able to visualize the scene. "Nope. I didn't once have the compulsion to toss my bones."

"Good, since I like heading to unique places to eat, and it'd be nice if you came with me."

I'd happily go almost anywhere with Gavin, and likely love every minute of it. I was having a love/hate relationship with my attraction to him, but he was nearly irresistible. Not that I thought he'd ever be interested in me as anything other than a friend. But honestly, I could use a companion who didn't see me as strange or boring.

He dropped several large bills on the table with the check the waitress had dropped off while we were eating.

"That's an enormous tip," I said without censoring my words.

"Dolores is a great waitress. I come here a lot, and she's always taken good care of me. Good service deserves compensation, and she has a kid in college. Can't be easy as a single mom."

My heart warmed at his thoughtfulness. Gavin obviously had no chip on his shoulder, despite his wealth. He'd greeted the waitress like a friend, hadn't expected special treatment, and paid her well as he left the table. So different from my father who treated hired help like his personal servants, and always complained that things weren't up to his demanding quality. "That was really nice of you."

Gavin stood and held out his hand. I grasped it and he pulled me up, though he was quick to wave off my comment. "I'm not that nice," he said, not letting my hand go as we made our way back to his vehicle.

When we were settled into the car, and he was headed toward a place to shop, I finally said what was on my mind. "Gavin?"

"Yeah?"

"There never has been and never will be anything bad about being a nice guy." In fact, his thoughtfulness was an amazing character trait.

Gavin was silent for a moment before he answered, "Charlie, I'm honestly not all that nice."

I ignored him. He *was* nice, but if he didn't want to admit to it, I'd be more than happy to keep his secrets just like he was keeping mine.

CHAPTER 9

Gavin

*F*ucking hell... I cursed myself as I finished our drive to the local mall in silence. I'd done time in the slammer, not once, *but twice*, and Charlie was under the impression I was some kind of hero because I'd slipped a few extra bucks to a woman in need.

I really needed to straighten her out, let her know that I was far from the sterling guy she imagined. I was one of the most tarnished individuals she'd ever meet.

As visions floated through my mind about what had happened with Kane when we were in prison, I cringed silently. What would my sweet Charlie think about the fact that I'd raped my best friend?

My attraction to her kept deepening to the point where my dick was constantly hard whenever she and I were in the same vicinity—which was all the time, at this point.

I wasn't sure what the hell was up with her father, but it sure as shit sounded like he wasn't exactly a proud parent. How in the hell could any man not be proud of a daughter like Charlie?

I wanted to fuck her, and I wanted that badly. But the problem was, I also really liked her, and that complicated everything. Charlie wasn't a woman you had a fling with and threw away. She was the type of woman you took to meet your family. She was the type of woman you spoiled. She was the type of woman a guy could fall for really hard.

And *that* made her dangerous.

There was no happily ever after for me, and certainly not with a woman like her.

I'd seen too much.

I'd done too much.

I'd experienced too much.

I had no doubt that some of the things I'd done she'd never understand. Why would she? Charlie had gone to school, studied to be a scientist, then pursued her career. Everything had been normal and above-board for her.

But I had lived my life in the shadows, and I stayed there. It was what I was used to, what I knew.

"What stores do you normally shop at?" I asked her. "Nordstrom?"

"Too expensive," she said as she shook her head. "I just need some casual stuff."

Nordstrom wasn't a store I considered expensive. At least, not anymore. There were plenty of luxury stores that were far more expensive to shop at.

We argued good-naturedly for a few minutes before I finally parked near the middle of the mall, and we made our way to the entrance. She could wander wherever she wanted and I'd follow her.

I grinned as she made a beeline for one of the cheapest stores in the mall, a place known for inexpensive, but good quality, casual clothing.

"Stock up," I warned her. "We don't know when all this will end."

She rolled her eyes, and the gesture was so damn cute that my dick was close to exploding.

"I do know how to do laundry," she informed me indignantly. "I don't need a whole bunch of stuff."

She took a cart, running up and down the aisles so efficiently it made my head spin.

Underwear.

Shoes.

Socks.

Jeans.

And then T-shirts and sweaters.

We came to the toiletries next, and she shoved a few things in the cart.

"I think that's it," she mused as she surveyed the items she'd gathered.

We'd been in the store all of twenty minutes, and if the store hadn't been so spread out, I'm sure she'd have managed to get everything done in five minutes flat.

"I've never seen a woman shop that fast," I said. "How in the hell did you do that?"

She shrugged. "Most of the stores are set up the same. I'm not much into shopping, so I get the things I need as I go. And I hate wandering around."

I knew instinctively that she was probably the type of woman who took a shopping list at Christmas and did everything in one, no-nonsense trip. Yeah, I kind of admired that, but it took the fun out of buying things for people who were important.

"Don't you ever look at other stuff?" I asked as she started pushing her choices to a cash register.

She looked at me in surprise. "Why? Then I'd just be tempted to impulse buy things."

"And that would be a bad thing?" I questioned.

"Of course. It would be a waste of time and energy, not to mention money."

I pushed my way to the pay center as she unloaded the items. Once she was finished, and everything was rung up, I swiped my card and put it away.

"We can't leave now," I complained as we walked out of the store.

"Why?"

"We haven't even been here for half an hour."

"Did you need to get something?" she questioned.

Actually, I didn't need a damn thing, but I took the bag from the cart as we dropped it at the door, then took her hand. "Let's window shop."

I wasn't completely certain, but I was pretty sure she shuddered as I led her down the line of stores. Her aversion to malls was actually pretty adorable.

In the next hour, I'd added a new phone, laptop, and several other items to her growing list of purchases.

"Gavin, I really don't need all of these things," she complained as we went to the car with the items.

"Yeah, you do. You need a secure way to contact the people in your life so that they don't worry about you when they realize you aren't around. And you need to be able to do that without having it get traced back to your location."

"There's only me and my father, and he isn't the type to panic," she stated matter-of-factly.

"Boyfriend?" Okay, the question wasn't totally necessary, but I needed to know for sure.

"Nobody," she answered wistfully.

I hated myself for being relieved that Charlie really *didn't* have much of a life, and in that respect, we were very much alike. Yeah, Kane or my siblings would put out the alert once they realized that I was MIA, but it would take a while. Otherwise, I pretty much didn't have anybody who gave a shit.

"What about your friends?"

She sighed as I opened the passenger door for her and she slid into the car. "There's nobody who cares enough to report my disappearance to the police. I pretty much have the kind of friends who meet up occasionally for lunch or dinner."

I slammed the passenger door and went to settle myself in the driver's seat. *Damn!* Charlie was really alone.

"You know, that's probably not the kind of thing you tell somebody you barely know," I told her, wondering what would have happened if I had wanted to harm her. "What if I decided I wanted to abduct you?"

She laughed. "If you wanted to take advantage of the situation, you would have already done it."

She was probably right, but she had no idea how difficult it was for me to fight the urge to pin her to the nearest wall and fuck her until my cock was satisfied.

Mine!

Fucking. Fantastic. I had it for Charlie in the worst of ways, and in addition to wanting to fuck her until she screamed my name, I wanted to take care of her, too.

There was no way I wanted her to know the internal battle I was fighting right now, but she sure as hell was not safe. If I heeded my baser instincts, she'd still be home in my bed trying to recover.

"Maybe so," I muttered simply, not wanting to continue this conversation.

All I wanted was for her to understand that she shouldn't trust me. She should *never* have faith in me. I wasn't the type of guy who deserved the respect of a woman like her.

"So where is your partner?" Charlie asked. "Does he know you're trying to save a damsel in distress?"

I was happy there was some levity in her voice. "He's on his honeymoon. He just got married. We're kind of between important projects at the moment."

That wasn't exactly true, but we weren't working on anything enormous. I had trials to do for a big company, but Kane wasn't as involved in testing as I was, and he deserved a damn honeymoon.

"So that's why you were playing on the dark web?" Charlie asked curiously.

"I want to dismantle as much of the dark web as possible," I explained. "If I could do it singlehandedly, I would. It's an interest of mine."

"An interest or an obsession?"

"Maybe a little of both," I admitted. "I fucking hate the shit that goes on there. Sex trafficking. Prostitution. Underground gambling. Hits on really nice female scientists."

She laughed, just like I'd hoped.

"I'm not much good on a computer," she explained. "I don't exactly hang out online and do the whole social media thing."

"You're not missing out on much—and the dark web is far different to anything most people would come across," I cautioned. "It's pure evil most of the time."

Nothing good ever happened on the dark web. Taking it down piece by piece was my personal mission.

"So you were cruising around on the dark web when you saw my hit?"

I flinched. "I saw it as I was looking around, yes." I hated the fact that I'd almost convinced myself not to get involved. So much bad shit happened there that I sometimes just focused on how I could abolish the whole thing rather than help one single person.

But somehow, Charlie's situation hadn't let me stay away.

"Thank you for stepping into this," she said quietly. "You certainly didn't have to. You may have saved my life."

As I pulled into my driveway, I acknowledged to myself that I was glad I had decided to take action. Just the thought of anything happening to Charlie made my whole body tense, and my protective instincts spring into action.

"It's not over yet," I warned her.

No, the situation was far from resolved, but I swore right then and there that nothing would ever happen to Charlie unless I was dead and helpless to protect her.

The bastards would have to go through me first.

CHAPTER 10
Charlie

The dogs ran around in an endless display of bliss as Gavin and I arrived back at his home. After they'd assured themselves that we weren't leaving again, they ran outside willingly, ready to play.

"I should check the net again," Gavin said calmly.

Personally, I was still freaked out over whether or not my boss had put the hit on me back up again.

I followed him to his office, and sat down on a small sofa to wait for him to investigate.

My body was tense as his fingers flew over his keyboard. And yet, despite it all, I couldn't help but admire Gavin, loving the intense concentration on his face as he looked for answers.

Gavin was absolutely brilliant. To have risen to the position he was in with his life right now, he had to be. The fact that he looked hotter than Hades when he was hell bent on doing something made him all the more attractive.

What would it be like to have that laser-sharp focus all on me?

Did Gavin even give his women the same attention that he gave his work?

If he was anything like me, he didn't, since I hadn't paid any guy any attention in ages.

Except when it came to Gavin. I'd happily focus on him.

"I'm surprised it's not back up, but I don't see it," Gavin observed.

"Thank God." My body shivered in relief.

"It could be that he already found his man," he explained. "I don't want to scare you by saying that, Charlie. I just don't want to give you a false sense of security. What the assholes are doing is extremely profitable, and they are playing for high stakes. This isn't just going to go away."

"I think I know that now," I acknowledged.

I might be naïve, but I wasn't stupid. I knew well enough the sort of prices our enemies would pay to have a biological weapon. When that large a sum of money was on the line, they wouldn't think twice about murdering someone standing in their way.

"You have to be careful," Gavin said in a concerned voice.

I sighed. "All of this over biological weapons. Why? That's one thing I just can't understand. As scientists, we work to find cures, so we can make the world a better place. Yes, we need to study dangerous diseases, but what American would sell out their country for money?"

"It's a lot of money," he said cynically. "Some people would sell their own family or they're fucking soul for that matter."

"I wouldn't," I answered. "We've seen pandemics, and studied the history of severe outbreaks. The Black Plague wiped out millions—half of the population of Europe. Even if somebody had money, what kind of world would they have to live in?"

Gavin shrugged. "Even knowing that, some people don't care. Money is king."

"Is that how you feel?" I asked curiously, pretty sure I knew the answer.

"Hell, no. Getting rich was never my objective, even if it was pretty important to my partner, Kane. But it wasn't just the money for him, either. He had something to prove. Maybe we both did."

"I'd hate to see a world where we couldn't contain another pandemic of epic proportions. Science has come way too far for that to happen. That's why we study. We're supposed to be looking for a cure, not killing people."

"I think almost every form of work can be studied for bad things," Gavin observed.

He was probably right. Even in the computer world, skills could be easily used for financial gain.

"We really need to end this, Gavin. We have to find a way to take these people down. The consequences of not getting biological weapons out of enemy hands could be catastrophic."

"I know," he replied. "We'll do everything we can. I'll use all the connections I've gotten over the years."

"What can I do?"

Before he could answer, a buzzing sound filled the room.

"Shit! Someone's at my gate, and I don't normally get visitors, especially when my partner is away, and I sent my sister and brother a note that I'd be out of town just so they didn't drop over." Instead of heading to answer the door, he tapped away on his keyboard, and just a moment later, he had the live feed from his front gate security camera up on his screen. "What the hell is *he* doing here? It's my contact at the FBI."

He tapped away again, remotely opening the gate, and then waiting to make sure the place was secure once again as the gate shut behind the agent. Gavin got to his feet, and grabbed my hand, leading the way to the front door, pulling it open and stepping aside so the agent could enter. "Lou... what the hell's going on? I hadn't expected you to come knocking," he said roughly. "This is Charlie. Charlie, this is special agent Louis Green."

"Our scientist." The FBI agent was a kind-looking African-American gentleman in his mid-fifties, who gave me a kind smile, and held out his hand. "Call me Louis or Lou."

I shook his hand, wondering why he was here. "If you're trying to help me, thank you," I rushed to tell him.

"You have my word, I'm doing all I can to put an end to the threat you're dealing with." Lou shifted his attention between me and Gavin. "Have you seen the news?"

"No. I've been too busy keeping Charlie safe," Gavin answered. "What's going on?"

"This is an ugly situation, and it just keeps getting worse," Louis told me.

"What did you find out?" Gavin asked.

"We've got trouble," the agent answered in a serious tone. "We aren't certain where this ends, yet, but we know it wasn't just some project being worked on by the lab supervisor."

"How do you know that?" I asked anxiously.

"Is your boss's name Doug Whitman?" Agent Green asked stoically.

"Yes. Dr. Whitman. He's been my superior as long as I've been at the lab," I confirmed.

"Was he supposed to be working today?" Louis asked.

"No. We run a really small crew on the weekends. No one in management comes in," I explained. I didn't even work weekends. It was a time when most of the mundane catchup was done by lab techs.

"He was there today," Louis commented. "Apparently he got there very early."

"Are you watching him? How did you know?" I was wondering why in the hell my boss was working in the early morning hours on a Sunday. That just never happened.

"Because the first one to come into the lab this morning found his body in his office. He was shot with a double-tap to the head. Dr. Whitman is dead."

CHAPTER 11

Gavin

This was *not* good news. Not at all. Because if Charlie's boss was dead, then it meant that whoever he was working for had decided that things had taken a turn they didn't like, and they were now looking to tie up loose ends.

And Charlie was one big ole loose end, and I had no doubt they were going to do all they could to make sure she didn't become an even bigger problem than she was now.

"Lou, above all, I need to keep Charlie safe. She's all that matters in this mess, especially when she hadn't realized what she was walking into." She'd been completely innocent—probably never did anything illegal in all her life—and now she had criminals hunting her down and wanting her dead. But there was no fucking way I was going to let that happen. "I can try to keep her safe on my own, but if the FBI can help in any way, I'll sure as hell be able to do a better job of it."

"We'll have to bring her in for questioning if we have any hope of keeping her out of harm's way. We need to figure out who's behind this, so we can try to put a stop to it at the source. And eventually, we'll also need her to testify if we have any hope of putting an end to this." Lou knew damn well that having her be a witness in this case, if it went to trial, would put a bull's eye on Charlie's back, and was already putting his hands up to try and calm me down. "I know you don't like the idea—and believe me, I get it. But the only way to make sure Charlie stays safe is to put these guys away for a very long time. And in order to do that, we need her help, though we'll do our best to work other angles."

I didn't just "not like" the idea — I fucking hated it. Yet I knew that Charlie's options were few, short of being on the run the rest of her life. And that just wasn't any way to live. "I want your word that if there's a way around getting her to testify, if there's some-one else who can testify in her place, especially when she only stumbled upon this by accident, then you'll go that route first."

"You have my word. But we're going to have to move quickly on this, and get her someplace safe. One person's already dead, and we still don't have any indication as to who's behind it. Though with Whitman's murder, we now have access to all his files and his home, even if there's a good chance that if the hit was done by a pro, they may have wiped Whitman's drives clean, and destroyed any evidence that would lead back to them." Lou shook his head, looking distracted with his thoughts. "Our teams are still trying to figure out whether or not they actually got their hands on the weaponized virus. If they did, it could be disastrous."

He was right. Depending on how they altered the virus, there may be no easy way to combat it, and it may have already fallen into the wrong hands. God only knew what they wanted it for or where they would use it, but the results would be the same.

People would die.

"They may have wiped his hard drives, but there's still a good chance that the data can be recovered. If you need my help in any way, just let me know. I want this over with as soon as possible." The faster we can get this over with, the safer Charlie would be. I reached over and gave her hand a squeeze, needing her to know that she wasn't alone in all this. "How are you holding up? Do you have any questions for Lou?"

"I don't know. I've never been in this kind of trouble before, and I honestly don't even know where to start. I'm in way over my head—if it weren't for you, I don't know what I'd do." She then turned her attention to Lou, looking visibly shaken up—and with her boss now dead, who could blame her? "I can't thank you enough for helping to keep me safe, and I don't want to sound ungrateful, but I can only go into hiding if I can bring my dog—and Gavin's dog too. After Ripley's time at the shelter, putting her in a kennel, no matter how nice, is just going to stress her out. I can't do that to her."

Lou's eyes flicked over to me in question, as if asking if she was actually serious. I put my arm around her shoulders in response. If that's what it took to get Charlie to agree to all this, then the dogs were coming with us—which suited me just fine. Though I could usually drop off Thor at my brother's place with no worries, given that my brother had no qualms about feeding Thor a steady diet of pizza crusts, steak grizzle, and any other table scraps that happen to be around, I liked that Charlie had immediately thought of the dogs. "You can't blame the girl for wanting to take care of her dog, now can you?"

Lou just shook his head, and gave us an easy smile. "No, I certainly can't. You know what my wife is like with our three dogs. Those pups are more spoiled than our kids are."

"I guess we should start packing." We'd only grab the essentials. Though I didn't know how long we would be gone for, we'd make do, or pick up what we needed once we got to wherever the hell we were going.

"I have men stationed outside your home. They'll take you to one of our safe houses when you're ready. Here's their number. Just let them know, and if you need anything at all, they can get in touch with me." Lou turned his attention back to Charlie.

"I appreciate your help with this matter, Charlie. You have my word—we'll do all we can to keep you safe."

I saw Lou to the door, noting that there weren't just two men stationed by my door, despite all my security, but that there were likely several more agents stationed around the perimeter of my property. Despite my past run-ins with the law, I had a good working relationship with the FBI, and given my hacking skills and my willingness to work with them, I knew they considered me an asset.

Did that mean they wouldn't have gone to all this trouble for Charlie alone? I didn't know, and frankly I didn't really care. All that mattered was that they'd go above and beyond to keep Charlie safe. She was my one and only concern in this mess, and I'd do whatever it took to make sure she got through it safely.

I resisted the urge to pull her into my arms again, knowing that I was already getting far too attached to her, and she deserved a hell of a lot better than anything I could offer her, given my past. "How are you holding up, love?"

"Honestly? I'm feeling rattled. *My boss is dead.* And though I know he was up to no good—and I haven't forgotten that he also put a hit out on me—it's still kind of hard to deal with the fact that someone who was in my life practically every day was violently murdered." She wrapped her arms around herself, as if warding off the chill, despite the comfortable temperatures.

Again, I had to fight the urge to cross to her side and pull her into my arms. I wanted to comfort her, and yet each touch, each moment spent in her company, took me down the path I wouldn't be able to return from, and I shouldn't be wandering down it in the first place. "I wish I could be more sympathetic towards him, but he tried to have you murdered, and he was weaponizing a virus that will likely go on to kill thousands of people if it ends up in the wrong hands."

She let out a ragged breath, looking shaken up. "I guess you never really know what people might be hiding. I couldn't have never imagined any of this."

Her words were like a knife to my heart. But they were exactly the reminder that I needed to keep my distance. I wasn't the man she thought I was. She may think I was some sort of knight in shining armor just because I'd managed to temporarily keep her from harm, but what would she think of me if she actually found out I'd raped my best friend while in prison? Hell, I was pretty sure just knowing I'd spent time in jail might possibly make her see me in a whole new light. The things I'd done that I wasn't proud of made up one hell of a long list, and I had no doubt she'd be appalled at the violence I'd committed.

I wasn't worthy of her. I just had to keep reminding myself of that.

"Come on. We should get packing. The sooner we can get you to a safe house, the better." I tried to put some distance between us, tried to put up some walls, but as smart as Charlie was, she immediately picked up on the change.

"I'm really sorry to be dragging you away from your life. You don't have to come with me, you know. I can manage on my own now that I have the FBI watching out for me. Not to say that I'm not grateful for everything you've done." Her words tumbled out in a hurry as her cheeks flushed red, her eyes refusing to meet mine. "I have no doubt I'd be dead right now if it weren't for you. But... I've already messed up your schedule and barged into your life. I'm sure you have work to do... things you'd like to get back to."

I fucking hated this. I needed to keep my distance, but pushing her away was only upsetting her, and making her think that she wasn't welcome here, that she was being a nuisance, when nothing could be further from the truth. For the first time since I could remember, I felt like I had finally found a bit of happiness...

found someone who could chase away my demons. Except that I wasn't worthy of her. I'd never be.

Yet I couldn't have her thinking that I didn't want her. So, despite everything I'd already told myself, I closed the distance between us and tipped her chin up so that she'd be forced to look at me. "The only thing that matters at the moment is *you*. Nothing else. There's nothing in my life that's more important than you and keeping you safe, and you have my word, I'll do whatever it takes to see you through this."

"I know you will. It's just hard not to feel like I'm in the way. Although... I guess maybe those are my hang-ups. My dad..." When her voice cracked, I had all too good an indication as to why she always seemed to be putting herself down, why she always seemed to be apologizing, or why she always seemed to think that she wasn't good enough.

And frankly, her father and I were going to have words, as soon as this mess was over. "I want you to forget about anything hurtful your father ever said to you, because it's clear he doesn't have a fucking clue as to just how sweet, smart, and kind you are. You're amazing, Charlie—and I hate that you'd think otherwise. A father's supposed to build you up—not tear you down."

"It's sweet of you to say that, but... things are complicated when it comes to my family. It's easy to blame my father for things, but there's a reason he is the way he is."

CHAPTER 12

Charlie

The last thing I wanted to do was talk about my family problems. I already had enough to contend with, and this was going to push me over the edge, even though I knew Gavin deserved to know the truth. "Please... just let it go, Gavin."

He looked so worried about me, which was damn sweet of him, even if just minutes earlier, it felt like he'd been putting some distance between us. "I'll let it go, love, even if I'm going to keep reminding you just how special you are."

His words and kindness had me going up onto my toes to kiss his cheek. "I don't think you'll ever know how much your words mean to me."

His eyes locked on mine, and he looked at me with such an intensity, it made my breath catch. It felt as though time stood still, the air between us crackling with a sexual energy that was impossible to ignore. I could hear my heart hammering away, and when he cupped my face in his hands and kissed me as if I was the very air he breathed, I felt his touch down to my very soul.

His fingers sinking into my hair as his tongue swept over mine, our kiss deepening as I let go of all my hang-ups, and tried to just live in the moment. Before long, Gavin was pulling away, even though he still held me close, our breathing heavy.

When he spoke, his voice was thick with need. "I know I probably shouldn't have done that, but at the moment, I can't say that I'm sorry. And if I'm being honest, I make no guarantees that I won't do it again."

Unable to resist him, and riding a high I had never felt before, I leaned in and stole just one more kiss, my lips pressed sweetly to his. "And I can guarantee that if you kiss me again, I won't stop you."

I'd never been so bold, but there was something about Gavin that made me feel different about myself—*and I liked it*. His words... his actions... they made me feel special. *He* made me feel special. And after nearly two decades of feeling like I wasn't good enough, of feeling like everything was my fault, it was damn nice not to have to carry that burden.

Because when Gavin looked at me, he saw the person I wanted to be, instead of the person I'd been told I was.

It didn't take me long at all to grab the few things I had, and with our bags packed and the dogs ready to go, I found myself tucked against Gavin's side as we rode off to some undisclosed location in an FBI vehicle, while the dogs settled down in the back of the massive bullet-proof SUV. It took us about three hours to get to where we were going, which turned out to be a good sized cabin buried up high in the mountains and surrounded by heavily wooded forests.

"The cabin has been fully stocked for you, and all the lines in and out of this place are secure. There's a vehicle in the garage, and you'll find new cell phones and laptops inside. If there's anything at all that you need, if there are any concerns you have, or any questions, don't hesitate to call us. We won't be far." Agent Latimer led the way to the cabin and got us settled while the others kept watch, but before long it was once more just me and Gavin and the dogs.

Gavin crossed to my side, his brow furrowed with worry. "How are you holding up, love? I know this is a lot to take in."

That was an understatement, since this felt a lot like some sort of witness protection program, albeit a temporary one. Add to that the little fact my boss had just been murdered and there was likely still a hit out on my life. "Honestly, I don't know. My life couldn't have been any more boring or normal. And now, I'm under FBI protection, someone wants me dead because of a weaponized virus I had nothing to do with, and I'm temporarily living with a man I've only just met, when I haven't even been on a date in close to a decade."

His lips quirked into a smile that lit up his blue eyes. "A decade, huh? Somehow I don't believe that."

"Okay. Maybe that's a *slight* exaggeration—but honestly, not by a whole lot. I work too many hours to ever get the chance to meet anyone, and other than the guys I work with, which are a definite no, or my pizza delivery guy, there's not a whole lot of opportunity. I mean, it took a hit on my life to get me to meet someone new. And last I checked, it's not exactly the best way to meet guys." I couldn't help but smile when he laughed, my mood improving drastically by simply having Gavin around.

"I don't know... I kind of like the whole damsel in distress dating method. And I'm all for strong powerful women who can kick ass, but I won't deny it's kind of nice to be able to save the day and be the hero, every now and then." With his hands stuffed in his pockets, he shrugged his shoulders and gave me another easy smile, so he looked not just sexy, but adorable—if a six foot three, muscular man, with smoldering sexy looks could be adorable.

"Well, there's no one else I'd rather have saving me when I'm in need of a hero." If I didn't know any better, I'd guess that I was actually flirting.

Me.

Flirting.

The world must be coming to an end.

I think I even managed to not look like a total idiot while doing so. Except, of course, that the mere thought of me flirting had my cheeks flaming with embarrassment. What the hell was I doing? Not that I could think straight with Gavin around.

"Sweetheart…" He brushed the back of his fingers against my hot cheek, his eyes locked on mine. "You're blushing."

"Am I?" A second wave of heat hit my cheeks as I pretended to be oblivious to the effect he had on me.

I wasn't sure what to say or do next. I was just so clueless, and clearly in way over my head. But before I could figure it out, Gavin grabbed my bag and snagged my hand. "Come on, love… let's check out our digs."

I forced myself to swallow down my disappointment, though I liked that he was, at the very least, maintaining some sort of physical contact between us.

Quaint and cozy was the best way to describe the cabin. With wooden beams vaulting the ceilings, shiplap on the walls, and a massive stone fireplace, I could just imagine sitting in front of the fire, curled up on the sofa, a snow storm raging outside as I snuggled up in Gavin's arms.

As if that was going to happen.

But still… a girl could dream. And if a girl was going to dream, she'd certainly be dreaming of someone just like Gavin, since he was nothing short of amazing.

Gavin dropped my bags in the master bedroom, taking the room across the hall from mine for himself, no doubt so he would be close by should I need him. As small as the home was, it didn't take us long to conclude our tour, finishing up on the back deck which overlooked the mountain ridge.

I turned to Gavin, grabbing his arm in my excitement. "It's just so gorgeous here. Though I lived in the country when I was younger, we never had views like this."

"The views really are stunning." But when I turned to face Gavin his eyes were on me, not on the view. Which of course had me blushing once again. He grabbed my hand and brought it to his lips before pulling me back inside and towards the kitchen. "I don't know about you, but I'm starving. Here's hoping they really did leave us a well-stocked fridge and pantry. They have no idea how much I can eat."

Luckily, they had. "Let me cook for you. What are you in the mood for?"

He groaned, his gaze drifting to my lips as he spoke, his voice gruff and sexy. "Sweetheart, what I'm hungry for isn't on the menu."

I wanted to tell him that he could have whatever he wanted—*happily*. And yet, who was I kidding? I didn't know the first thing about men. I was totally inexperienced, and Gavin was *way* out of my league, even if we seemed to have a fair few things in common. But there was a reason I happily stayed holed up in my lab, and that was because I was clueless when it came to being social. Everyone always thought of me as quiet and mousy, even though I knew there was more to me than what others saw.

And if my own parents had never even seen me for who I was, what hope did I have of getting others to.

I shook myself free of my thoughts—and pushed away my father's voice from my head as his words started to weasel their way into my head. I was getting damn tired of not living up to expectations that were impossible to meet. I was never going to be able to take my brother's place. So why bother?

Knowing that Gavin would likely eat anything I put in front of him, I started pulling out ingredients. "Why don't you get a fire going in the fireplace, and I'll get started on dinner?"

"I guess that'll have to do—for now."

CHAPTER 13

Gavin

Charlie was making it damn hard for me to keep my distance, despite knowing that no good could come of pursuing this, given my past. Yet here I was, pulling her close and kissing the tip of her nose, before forcing myself to let her go.

There was just something about her that muddled my thoughts, so I found myself running on pure need, overwhelming attraction, and simply liking her way too much, my good intentions falling to the side the moment she was near.

I had to do better. Because there was no way she deserved to be with someone who had such a messed up past, and had not only been to prison but had been forced to rape his best friend. And though that may not have been my fault, given the drugs they'd given us, and the knife they'd held to our throats, I'd still gone through with it, and for that, I could never forgive myself, even if Kane didn't blame me.

If I was going to pursue Charlie in any way shape or form, then she would need to know the truth, and frankly, that wasn't a secret I was in any mood to tell. That meant pursuing Charlie just wasn't an option.

Needing to keep myself busy and away from Charlie, I got to work building a fire in the massive stone fireplace, even if my mind continued to drift back to her. Trying not to think about her was impossible, especially when we were going to be living together for the foreseeable future. And this quaint and cozy cabin felt far too romantic, making it even harder to keep my distance.

I added another log to my pile and stuffed kindling between the openings as I stole a glance in her direction. She'd never been in this particular kitchen before, yet she looked completely at ease as she moved around, looking in the cabinets and opening the drawers to find what she needed. I didn't know what she had planned for dinner, but if I had to guess, it'd be nothing short of amazing, just like her. And it was damn hard not to picture her looking completely at home at my own place—a place we could make ours.

Once I got the fire going, I crossed to her side, unable to stay away even as I chastised myself for being an idiot, knowing I was setting myself up for one hell of a hard fall. Not that it mattered at the moment. All I could think of was closing the distance between us, and putting a smile on her face—and if it involved her screaming out my name as I made her come, then all the better.

I may be a nice enough guy, if one was willing to ignore my past, but it didn't mean I was a goddamned monk. And Charlie? She was just too fucking perfect to pass up, making it impossible for me to keep my distance.

"I don't know what you're cooking, but it already smells damn good." I tried to stay out of her way as I leaned against the counter, needing to be close. "Anything I can do to help?"

"I think I've got it under control. Though it's nothing fancy—I can guarantee you that. I enjoy cooking, but it's always just a bit of this and that. And I hate to admit it, but sometimes it works, and sometimes it doesn't." She tossed me a charming smile over her shoulder as she sliced up some mushrooms and tossed them in a large pan where she was already sautéing some leeks and chicken. "Don't suppose you can see if they left us a bottle of wine? It's not a problem if there isn't. It's just that it'll be tastier if I can add it."

"Let me see here..." After poking around in a handful of the kitchen cabinets, I spotted a wine rack over by the dining area. Luckily, they'd left us with a decent selection. "Would you prefer white or red?"

"White, if you have it."

I did. I grabbed a decent bottle, and a few glasses while I was at it, and headed back to her side, pulling the cork and pouring us a generous amount before handing her the bottle and sliding her glass over. "Here you go, love."

"Thanks." She splashed some wine in and gave it all a stir, and then emptied a box of pasta into the pot of boiling water, before tossing me a hesitant smile. "Being up here in the mountains, away from it all—being here with you—it's easy to forget that someone wants me dead."

Fuck. She was totally right. Being here, in the safety of an FBI safe house, had us letting down our guard and relaxing, making it far too easy to forget why we were here in the first place. "I know what you mean. But I swear, we'll find out who's behind this and put an end to it."

"I just feel bad that you've gotten dragged into my mess. If anything ever happened to you, I swear, I'd never forgive myself." She glanced away as her eyes filled with tears.

"Hey..." I tipped her chin towards me with a gentle touch, only to find her tears rolling down her cheeks, catching me off guard that she'd be this upset about it. "Nothing's going to happen to either of us. You have my word. I'm going to keep you safe."

"It's not me I'm worried about—*it's you.* I can't bear the thought of something happening to you. It's my fault you've gotten mixed up in this to begin with." She shook her head, her gaze wandering, clearly still upset and leaving me to wonder if there was more to it than just what was happening here between us.

Cupping her face in my hands, I brushed her tears away and kissed her sweetly, needing her to know that she wasn't alone... that I wasn't going to let anything happen to her, even if it was me she was worried about. "I don't want you worrying about any of this. And, Charlie... if there's anything you need to talk about, if there's anything I can do to help see you through this, I'm here for you."

All I could do was hope that, in time, she'd trust me enough and feel comfortable enough around me to open up and tell me what had her looking so haunted. Because there was something she wasn't telling me... something in her past that had truly messed with her head. And if I had to guess, her father was involved.

"I'm sorry about the tears. I think it's all just catching up with me." She managed a halfhearted smile and turned back to cooking, no doubt using it as a distraction to keep from having to discuss the matter.

Before long, the dogs were munching away on their dinner, and we were sitting down to a hearty meal of creamy chicken and pasta in one of the tastiest sauces I'd ever had, opting to sit in front of the cozy fire, instead of the dining room table. "Damn, Charlie. You can really cook. This is fantastic."

Looking proud, she beamed at me, her smile lighting up her eyes and making me one hell of a happy man, now that she was no longer haunted by whatever the hell it was that kept creeping its way to the surface. "I'm so relieved that you like it. Cooking's become a bit of a hobby now that I'm living on my own in Seattle. I don't tend to get out too much, aside from dog walks, so it's been good for killing time, especially on the weekends. And since I'm alone, I usually have leftovers to carry me through the week and I'm busy with work."

It shouldn't feel this damn good to hear that she was all alone, but I hated the thought of another man in her life. I wanted her all to myself, even if I knew I shouldn't go there.

I'd never felt this way about anyone else, which was making it damn hard for me not to pursue her. Yet even if I came clean to her about my past, that didn't change what I'd done. We may seem perfect for each other, but nothing could chase away my demons, and she deserved a whole lot better than me.

Now all I had to do is keep my distance.

I scoffed at myself. As if I'd even come close to managing that with Charlie around.

CHAPTER 14

Charlie

Though I didn't normally drink, my nerves were getting the better of me with everything that was going on, and the wine seemed to be helping with that. At the very least, it was letting me relax around Gavin, since being anywhere remotely near him sent my heart skittering out of control.

No one else had ever had that sort of effect on me, which was why I must be Seattle's oldest virgin. My nose had always been buried in a textbook, even when I was younger, and the guys didn't usually go for the geeky type when there were cheerleaders around. And then, once I had finished with my studies, I was too busy with work to bother dating – and it's not like there was anyone around worth dating, anyway. I certainly wasn't the type to go to a bar to pick up men, and most of the guys I worked with were already taken and often times much older than me.

But Gavin? Gavin couldn't be any closer to perfect. Looks, personality, attitude… he had it all, and then some, since he wasn't just amazing, he was also sweet and caring and smart. He checked off every box in the ideal boyfriend category.

Yet, despite the signals he was sending, there was no way this was anything more than a fantasy. And once this threat was over, he'd go back to his life and I'd go back to mine.

I finished off my glass of wine, and though it may not be a great idea, I didn't stop Gavin when he refilled my glass. For once, I just wanted to enjoy myself, and I knew the wine would quiet my racing thoughts and insecurities.

Before long, we were done with dinner, though it was still early enough in the evening. Gavin insisted on making quick work of the dishes, and eventually, we ended up curled up on the sofa, where we'd been eating dinner.

I shifted to face him, taking another sip of my wine, his intense gaze making me far too nervous. He was already so close, our knees brushing. The air between us seemed electrified with the delicious tension that had me wanting to lean in and kiss him again.

Maybe it was the wine... maybe it was the fact that there was a hit out on my life and suddenly whatever time I had left on this earth seemed precious and not to be squandered... But I found myself leaning forward and brushing my lips against his, my kiss filled with all the uncertainties I had about myself.

Gavin deepened our kiss, his fingers slipping into my hair as he pulled me to him, his tongue sweeping over mine in a delicious dance that had me climbing into his lap, my legs straddling his thighs as my hips rocked up against his impossible to ignore erection. I'd never, in all my life, been so bold. But then again, never had anyone had this sort of effect on me.

Never had anyone even come close to being Gavin.

I was so desperate for him, but it seemed as if my body had a mind of its own, my hips rocking to their own rhythm—a rhythm he matched—as our kiss grew more fervent.

But then, he was breaking away from me with a groan, though he didn't pull away, his head still bent to mine and my face still cupped in his hands. "Sweetness... you're making it damn hard for me to behave myself."

"I've always behaved, Gavin. Always tried to do the right thing, always tried to play by the rules. And where the hell has it gotten me in life? My brother's dead, my entire family hates me because of it, and I now have a hit out on my life, forcing me to hide out under FBI protection." My words all came tumbling out before I could stop them, and though I hadn't wanted to mention my brother and my parents, it felt good to get it out there for once.

"Charlie... I'm so sorry about your brother." He brushed his thumb over my cheek, his touch gentle as my eyes burned with threatening tears.

"I shouldn't have said anything." I started to pull away from him, but he gripped my hips and held me there so I had no choice but to stay and deal with what I'd started. "It was a long time ago. When we were kids. But... I guess some wounds never heal."

"No, love. They don't. Especially not if you continue to beat yourself up about it." There was a sincerity in his voice, a pain there, that caught me off guard. "You said your parents blamed you... What happened, Charlie?"

I shook my head no, not wanting to tell him. Even though I relived that nightmare every day... *every night.* It was buried so deep inside me, I didn't think I could pull it free from my darkest depths, even if I tried.

"I can't..." My tears finally broke free, slipping down my cheeks as I was helpless to stop them. "I can't talk about it. I'm so sorry, Gavin."

"Hush, love... it's okay. You don't have to talk about it if you don't want to." He looked so worried about me as he wiped my tears from my cheeks with a gentle sweep of his thumbs, my face cradled in his hands, before he held me to him.

Nestled against him, I rode out my emotions in the safety of his arms, no longer feeling alone for the first time in as long as I could remember. I'd blamed myself for so long, but with my father constantly reminding me that it was my fault that my brother was gone, I had no hope of ever healing and moving past it.

I was exhausted from carrying the weight of that burden, even if it was mine to carry. Yet being with Gavin... It was as if he'd somehow taken that burden from me, the weight no longer suffocating me. I knew my time with Gavin was only temporary, but I wanted to make the most of my time with him.

With my emotions finally under control, it quickly became apparent that both our bodies were well aware of the fact that I was still straddling his lap. I pulled away just enough to be able to look at him, but that only led to my hips shifting against his already steel-hard erection. I bit back the needy moan that wanted to escape my lips, though it took all I had not to rock my hips against his cock, in search of relief.

I'd never felt this close to anyone, even though I knew how insane that was, given my age. A lot of that had to do with the fact that I'd shut everyone out and put walls up around myself, not thinking myself worthy of any happiness, when my brother would never get to live his life. Yet Gavin had managed to tear down my defenses, and instead of feeling vulnerable around him, I felt whole for the first time in a *very* long time.

My eyes locked on his, and once again, the air between us crackled with a sexual tension that was impossible to ignore. Despite my problems and my past—or maybe because I finally wanted to move past them—I found myself wanting to throw caution to the wind.

I wanted Gavin.

He must have read my thoughts because before I could find my courage, his mouth found mine in a hungry kiss that set my body alight with a need I couldn't ignore. He tangled his fingers through my hair, deepening our kiss as I moaned into his mouth, my hips rocking against his hard cock as my body pressed against him in a desperate search for some relief.

Never had I felt like this... so alive... so wanted... *so at peace.* And at the moment, I could think of nothing but giving myself to Gavin, even if I was nervous about it being my first time.

Yet who could possibly be more caring, more understanding, more loving than Gavin? The answer was no one. And for just a few hours, I wanted to live a life that wasn't mine, away from my never ending nightmare.

I wanted Gavin to be my first.

CHAPTER 15

Gavin

F ucking hell… Any hope I'd had of keeping my distance evaporated in the heat of our scorching kiss. The weight of her body as it pressed against my hard cock made it impossible for me to think straight. I didn't stand a chance when it came to resisting her, and at this point, I didn't want to.

I'd make amends for my past sins, and come clean about the life I'd led, once I'd quenched my need for her, even if I didn't think it possible that I'd *ever* get my fill. But none of that was more than a fleeting thought when I was kissing her and holding her close.

She broke from our kiss just long enough to pull her top up over her head, and if I'd thought that resisting her was hard before, it was nothing compared to now. "Sweetheart… you're not making this easy on me."

Almost as if she was too shy about me seeing her partially naked, she pressed herself against me, her lips on mine as she spoke between sweet kisses. "I swear, I've never done anything like this before. *Ever.*"

There was something in her voice that had me doing a bit of a double take. A hesitation… an insecurity… almost as if…

No... She couldn't be.

I pulled away just enough to be able to look her in the eyes, brushing a lock of her hair from her face. "Sweetness... when you say you've never done this before, you mean... *you've never had sex?*"

Her cheeks flushed scarlet, giving me all the answers I needed. *Fucking hell...*

"Charlie... I don't know what to say." Especially since this definitely meant that there was no way I could go through with any of this. I shouldn't have gone down this road to start with—and now there was even more reason to put a stop to this. There was no way I could be her first.

"Then don't say anything. Just, please... I've never felt this comfortable with anyone else before. And if not you, then it feels like it may never happen." She bit her bottom lip, looking fucking adorable, even if I hated the worry in her eyes. "I like you, Gavin—like I've never liked anyone before. Or... is it that you don't like me that way? Oh my god... have I been reading this wrong all along?"

She tossed her top back on and tried to get off my lap, mumbling her apologies, but I wasn't letting her go anywhere. Wrapping my arm around her waist, I pulled her back to me, securing her there on my lap. "Don't run, sweetheart. You definitely haven't been reading me wrong. I'm sorry about how this all played out. It just caught me a bit off guard."

The last thing I wanted to do was hurt her feelings or make her feel even more uncomfortable, though it left me in one hell of a bind. Every fiber of my being wanted to pursue this thing with her. Yet I'd be nothing but an ass if I didn't first tell her about my past, and I wasn't sure that was a story I was ready to tell.

I still hadn't truly dealt with what I'd done or the consequences of my actions, and as horrible as it was, I wasn't sure I could get the words out and tell her that, not only had I been in prison, but that I'd raped my best friend.

How the hell could I tell her that?

Frankly, I wasn't sure I could. But that also meant that I couldn't pursue this any further, no matter how badly I wanted to—and no matter how badly she wanted me to also. I hated disappointing her, but better to live with her disappointment than with her hate. And it had nothing to do with Kane being another man, but everything to do with the heinous act of me violating him, and taking him against his will. How could anyone forgive me or look past the fact that I'd raped someone, even if I'd been drugged and my life threatened?

Charlie pulled me from my thoughts, and I gladly turned my attention back to her, rather than deal with my demons. "I know we've only just met each other, but I really do like you, Gavin. And I'm not saying we have to rush into this and have sex, but…" She let out a weary sigh, the light in her eyes dimming. "I guess it was silly of me to think that you'd be interested."

"That's where you're wrong, Charlie. Any man would be lucky to have you — me included. You're nothing short of amazing. But… I'm not a nice man, and I've done not so nice things. Frankly, you deserve a hell of a lot better than me." I bent my head to hers so I could see her eyes, needing her to know what she meant to me. "I'm doing this to protect you. Because the last thing I'd ever want to do is hurt you in any way."

"I can't imagine you'd ever hurt me, Gavin. After all, you're the one who saved me. You've gone well out of your way to make sure I'm safe and that I'm not freaked out, and I can guarantee most guys wouldn't have even bothered with anything more than contacting the police." She slipped her arms around my neck, and then nestled her head in the crook of my neck, my heart hammering away as I held her to me. "I'm just not sure how I can move on from this, on my own, especially now that I know what it's like to have you at my side, watching my back."

I kissed the top of her head, running my hand down over her hair, trying to soothe her. "You're not alone, baby girl. I've got you. And I'm not going anywhere."

It felt like something was shifting between us, something far greater than probably either of us had anticipated — and it was probably something we both desperately needed in our lives. Except that it was clear we both had demons we were wrestling with.

But maybe, if we gave this a little more time... maybe we would be able to find a way to open up to each other and be honest—maybe then, we might stand a glimmer of a chance of finding some way to make this work. And yet I knew that I was just being stupidly hopeful, because the thought of having to walk away from Charlie felt impossible.

"I'm not giving you up, Charlie... but maybe we just need to take things slow. Get to know each other better... And then maybe, once we've put our demons to rest, things will be easier." If she didn't hate me for the horrible things I'd done.

She pulled away just enough to look at me, her eyes searching my face as worry furrowed her brow. "Gavin... If there's ever anything you need to talk about... I'm here for you. It never occurred to me that someone who was so put together might have their own demons to deal with. But I guess, we all have a past. Don't we?"

"I'm afraid so."

CHAPTER 16

Charlie

*I*t never occurred to me that Gavin might be dealing with his own issues. And clearly, whatever he was dealing with had certainly had an effect on him, especially since it felt like that was the reason he was holding back. I may be pretty clueless when it came to these sorts of things, but I'd be hard-pressed to deny that there was an attraction between us, and it wasn't just one sided.

Most guys wouldn't have hesitated for even a moment, given how willing I'd been to take things further. So unless I was completely mistaken, and Gavin didn't find me at all attractive, then that meant there was something else going on. And he'd said as much when he mentioned his demons and trying to work through his past.

Gavin seemed so sweet and smart, so put together... I couldn't imagine what he was dealing with, though it was clear he wasn't ready to talk to me about it. And why should he? It's not like he'd known me for long. Hell... I'd never even heard his name or said hello to the guy just days earlier.

"I've got an idea." Gavin gave me a smile, and though I knew he was likely just trying to change our mood around, I was grateful for it. "When we were first pulling up to the cabin, I spotted some Adirondack chairs on the back patio. What do you say to watching the sunset? It will also give the dogs a chance to play outside."

I grinned from ear to ear, stealing a quick kiss, and loving his thoughtfulness. "I think it's a perfect idea. Unless… it's not safe." Given that I've never been in this sort of situation before, I didn't know exactly how secure this location was, and though I'd like to get out and watch the sunset and try and put my embarrassment behind me, I'd rather not get my head blown off.

"This should be a completely secure location. No one knows we're here, and the FBI are going to make sure that it stays that way." He tucked a lock of my hair behind my ear, the gesture so sweet, it immediately had my heart racing for him, and there was no denying how drawn I was to him.

Maybe it had to do with the lack of any real affection that I got from my parents after my brother's death. But I craved Gavin's touch, and if I had to guess, I'd say it had more to do with Gavin and the effect he had on me, versus me just being lonely.

Unable to resist, I leaned in and pressed my lips to his one last time before climbing out of his lap, the dogs immediately perking up and getting to their feet from where they'd been lounging by the fire.

He stood by my side, towering over me, as his body brushed up against mine, almost as if we couldn't bear to be apart. "I doubt we'll be long, given how cold it is. We can leave the fire going since it's safe enough, and that way we can warm back up quickly once we get back in."

Grabbing my hand, he led the way to the back porch, the roof overhead keeping the chairs from being snow-covered. There was a definite chill to the air, which left me grateful that Gavin had grabbed the throw off the sofa, and there was a two-seater that we could snuggle up on. The dogs ran down into the yard, excited to play, and luckily, well behaved enough not to take off on us.

I curled up by Gavin's side, as we snuggled under the throw, his arm draped over my shoulder, and I honestly couldn't think of anything more perfect. The setting sun painted the sky in pinks and oranges, as a midnight blue seeped in from above, the sky changing from moment to moment. It truly was beautiful, and I couldn't think of anyone more perfect to spend the evening with. I knew I must be insane to be growing so attached to someone I'd only just met, but Gavin felt like my kindred spirit and our bond had been immediate.

The sun had nearly set when the dogs perked up and became alert at something — which immediately had Gavin stiffening at my side and sitting up, ready to go after an attacker should he need to. But then he relaxed, sitting back once more as he leaned into me and pointed towards the tree line. "Right there, love... Do you see it?"

A huge deer stood hidden amongst the trees, alert and ready to bolt. But once it spotted the dogs, it was clear it wouldn't be hanging around for long. Just as quickly as it came, it was off again, though its brief presence left me feeling far more at peace.

My life may be a mess, but I still had things to be grateful for, and I was going to make the most of them.

My nightmares were always the same.

The ice cold water stealing my breath as I tried to break to the surface...

The numbing cold that kept my limbs from working...

The weight of my winter jacket... my snow pants... my snow boots, weighing me down like lead. I tried to fight the pull of gravity as it threatened to drown me in the cold icy lake.

Jessie, just seven years old at the time and only two years younger than me, had run out onto the ice. I called out to him, trying to get him to come back, knowing we weren't allowed to go on the lake.

But he didn't want to listen.

Our parents would be so angry with us if they found out. I had to get him back.

I hated going onto the ice, but he was already a good distance away, and I had to get him off the lake. The further away I got from shore, the slower and more careful I became, even as I continued to yell at him, begging him to come back. Finally, my brother stopped and looked over at me, but it was only to mock and tease me, like he always did. "Chicken. You're always so worried about everything, and you never want to have any fun."

I wanted to tell him that it wasn't true. That I had plenty of fun, and he was just being mean.

Before I could say anything, there was a sudden look of shock on his face—and then Jessie was gone, falling through the ice. I screamed out his name and started to run towards him as he broke through to the surface, scrambling to try and get some sort of hold so he could pull himself out. Yet there was nothing for him to hold onto... no way to pull himself out. Each time he tried, another chunk of ice broke off.

I had to reach him but he was still so far away. Someone else calling to us... *help was on its way.* I quickly waved them down, and then turned back to run to Jessie, when the ice gave out from under my feet.

The icy cold water seized my lungs and stole my breath as I plunged into the deep dark lake, stealing my scream. I struggled to survive, struggled to get to the surface, kicking with all my might. I managed to steal a desperate breath as I broke through to the surface, my limbs flailing... and then the darkness of the lake was swallowing me whole once again, the fight going out of me as I ran out of breath...

The next thing I knew, strong arms were pulling me out of the water, just enough for me to finally catch my breath, my rescuer sprawled out on the ice as he held onto me, while others tried to make their way to us safely, so they could pull us to the shore.

I tried to scream out to Jessie... tried to tell them to leave me and go help my brother... but my words were frozen in my throat.

And my brother? *My brother was gone.*

It was still early in the morning, but staying in bed and trying to sleep in was pointless when sleep would only lead to more nightmares. And any sleep I did get wasn't the kind that would actually put a dent in my exhaustion. Instead it was fraught with tossing and turning as my mind raced.

I padded out into the kitchen, feeling miserable after my restless night. Though I should be surprised to find that Gavin was already up at such an early hour, I was starting to think he slept even less than I did.

"Sweetness... what are you doing up already? You should be sleeping. The sun's still hours from rising." He set aside his laptop and patted the spot on the sofa next to him.

I sat down by Gavin's side and curled up against him, taking comfort in the peaceful calm his strong arms afforded, grateful that I now had him in my life. With his arms draped around my shoulders, he enveloped me in their safety as I breathed in his scent, one deep breath after another, a calm slowly settling over me as he worked a magic he probably didn't even know he could wield.

"What's wrong, love? Something's clearly bothering you." He already knew me so well. Better than even my parents did after a lifetime of living with me. Though maybe that had more to do with the fact that Gavin actually cared about me, and my parents... my parents hadn't.

I somehow managed a smile as I looked up into his bright blue eyes. "It's nothing. I think it was being in a new place... a new bed. Usually it takes me a few nights to adjust. Though maybe... if I had company, I might sleep better."

He groaned out loud, making me laugh. "Don't tease me, girl. I'm trying to be good here—and you're making it damn hard."

I leaned into him, whispering in his ear. "Then maybe being good is overrated."

CHAPTER 17

Gavin

I'd been exposed to a lot of temptation in my life, but Charlie was the only one that I wouldn't and couldn't indulge in.

Holy fuck!

She was a virgin. A beautiful innocence that I wanted nothing more than to claim as mine.

Our chemistry was undeniable, but the problem was, I really liked her, respected her for the intelligent, caring woman that she was. A guy didn't take advantage of that, especially not one who wasn't the least bit worthy of being the first man to be with her.

Damn! Why did that idea make me want to scoop her up and drag her to a cave somewhere?

I couldn't take her, but I sure as hell didn't want another guy touching her, either.

"You know I want you. But I can't, Charlie. As much as I'd like to, it's not possible. There are too many things you don't know about me." I was afraid if she knew the truth, she'd never look at me again the way she was right now.

She thought I was some kind of hero, and she couldn't be more misinformed.

Charlie put a comforting hand on my arm, and that simple touch almost broke me. I squeezed her more tightly in my arms, knowing that I could never have anything more than her body cuddled sweetly against mine.

"Then tell me, Gavin. There's nothing you could ever say that would change my mind. I'm not a virgin because I want to be, or because I've been saving myself. I've just never felt this kind of attraction before. You're the only one who makes me feel this way," she confided breathlessly.

Shit! Shit! Shit! I needed to move away from her, but I couldn't. The only way I was moving is if I shocked her into moving someplace else.

Mine! The thought of her pulling away, rejecting me, made my gut ache.

"You want to know about my past? You want to know the real me?" I growled.

"I *already* know you," she answered. "But would I like to know what's bothering you? Yes."

I stared straight ahead at the wall, not wanting to see her look of disappointment while I spoke. "I grew up hard," I shared. "My siblings and I never had a childhood. We spent most of our time trying to stay alive in a world of violence while living on the wrong side of the tracks."

"Then it's all the more admirable that you've gotten to where you are in life," she said reasonably.

I laughed, a bitter sound with no humor. "You won't think so once you've heard the whole story. A lot of things happened between then and now. I was desperate for money so we could all get out of poverty. My mom was already working three jobs, but it just wasn't enough. As the oldest, I knew I had to help, and our only chance was using my computer skills to make some cash."

"You just did what you had to." As always, she was trying to see the good in me, when I knew better.

"I'm a hacker, Charlie. I've always been a hacker, even though I was running a PC that I'd put together with salvaged parts, and I had no formal training or college. But I was good, and so I used my skills to make money. At first, it was petty stuff, but it made me enough cash to provide better for my family. Unfortunately, at the time I wasn't sophisticated enough to cover my tracks. I've served two sentences for hacking. I was better at it the second time around, and it took a while for them to catch me, but I eventually got sent back to prison."

Charlie was completely silent for a while, like it was taking some time for that information to sink in. Finally, she answered, "Did you steal from people?"

I shrugged. "Tiny amounts from tons of accounts. I never wanted to do much damage to any one person. But eventually I was caught."

"You haven't gone back again?"

I shook my head. "I met Kane the second time I was in prison. We bonded together for protection at first, though we quickly learned we could trust each other. He was in for manslaughter... Things went wrong when he tried to protect his younger brother from thugs."

"What happened after that?" she asked in a hushed tone.

"Kane and I finally grew up and went legit. Well, as honest as a hacker can be. When we were both out, we founded our company. It's taken years for us to get where we are, but we're a great team."

"Gavin, it's not a crime to try to support your family. Desperate times sometimes require desperate behavior. You've paid for what you did. Why can't you give yourself credit for going straight?" She threaded her fingers through my hair and stroked the locks to comfort me.

"*Don't you get it?* Because what I did was *wrong,* and I *still* bend the rules. It's just usually being done trying to assist the authorities now."

"Like trying to eliminate the atrocities that are happening on the dark web?"

"Some of it," I grumbled.

"I think knowing where you came from makes me admire you even more," she mused. "I've never had to worry about where my next meal was coming from. My physical needs were taken care of." She laid her head on my chest with a trust that nearly made me come undone.

I knew what Charlie was saying was true. She obviously came from a much wealthier background than I did, but I had a feeling she had problems just as serious as my own.

"I was branded a criminal, Charlie. And I always will be. No matter what happened after those prison stints, I'm still a convict. You understand why I can't sleep with you? I'm a hardened bastard."

"Maybe I like men with character," she said defensively. "It doesn't matter that you fell, it just matters that you rose up again to fight in a better way."

"It isn't just that," I rumbled irritably. "Shit happens in prison, things that stay with a person forever. Situations and regrets I can never change."

She scooted closer to me. "Just tell me, Gavin."

I blew out a deep breath. "Friendships and alliances are formed in prisons... prison gangs. Kane and I stuck together because the last thing we wanted was to have to deal with crazy murderers and career criminals. Neither of us was in for long. We just needed to survive long enough to get the hell out of there. And when we did get out, we were determined to change our lives for the better. We stuck together to keep the gangs off our backs. But being two men who were willing to scrap wasn't always enough. Their gangs were bigger, and more powerful. Our release dates were pretty close, and we knew we just had to get through a few more months when something bad happened. Really bad."

Tormented visions flashed across my mind and I cringed as I relived what I'd done to Kane. My gut rolled as guilt flooded over me.

"What happened, Gavin?" She gave my hand a squeeze, letting me know it was okay... that she'd be there for me.

"There was one gang in particular that hated us. They knew the best way to weaken us was to turn us against each other—except whatever they'd tried hadn't worked. It just made us stronger, bonded us closer. Until one of them came up with the most twisted and sadistic idea."

"What did they do?"

"They managed to drug us and then caught us in an ambush. I think Kane and I both figured we were dead because we were hopelessly fucked up from the drugs—the ecstasy they'd slipped into our food. The bastards had knives and nothing to lose, since they were lifers. Kane and I were both strung out on drugs and adrenaline."

I stopped, my breathing ragged as I tried to gather my courage to tell Charlie my secret, something I'd never discussed with anybody except Kane.

"It's okay, Gavin. I could never hate you," she reassured me.

"Oh yeah, you could," I argued. "But nobody will ever hate me as much as I hate myself. What I did that day fucking haunts me."

"Did they hurt Kane?" she guessed.

"They beat the crap out of both of us," I explained. "I was so high on the drugs they'd slipped us that it didn't matter. I couldn't tell right from wrong, and I hated the fact that I had no control to fight."

"It wasn't your fault," Charlie protested.

"Actually, the worst part of it *was* my fault. I may have been forced, but I should have died before I did what they made me do to my best friend."

"Tell me," she pleaded.

"After they beat us up, they insisted that I fuck Kane. They knew it'd be the best way to make us hate each other. Between the knives to our throats, and being so screwed up on the ecstasy, I did it. I did the most horrible thing I can think of, Charlie. I raped my best friend."

CHAPTER 18

Charlie

My heart clenched, the pain in my chest unbearable as I listened to Gavin's confession. I was momentarily shocked. I couldn't deny that I was surprised by what had occurred. But it wasn't because it happened. I was appalled that it could happen in a prison where guards would generally be everywhere.

I cuddled closer to him, my heart breaking for the guilt and pain it must have costed him to live with what he'd done to Kane. He was still tormented, still locked in another kind of prison that he'd never managed to escape.

"Where the hell were the guards?" I asked furiously.

"They got paid off to be elsewhere. Happens more often than you'd think. Luckily, someone finally came through before the assholes could slice us up or kill us."

His big body shuddered, and I knew his pain was still there. He was still suffering.

"What happened with Kane?"

I couldn't think of a more horrible position to be in than to have to hurt a friend just to stay alive.

"I hurt him," Gavin mumbled. "Both physically and mentally. But he got over it. He understood why it happened, and didn't blame me. But it still took us a while to get back to the way we were before it happened. Kane tells me all the time that I need to get over my guilt, and that it wasn't my fault. He's moved on. I've tried, but I just don't think I can ever get past the fact that I betrayed him that way. If I hadn't been drugged out of my mind, I never could have gotten it up enough to even have it happen."

"He forgave you, Gavin. I think it's time for you to forgive yourself. Kane's right. It wasn't your fault. And I think everybody you know, including me, is glad that you're still alive." Just the thought of him being killed made my blood run cold.

"Kane's married now, and happy. I don't think he really thinks much about his past," I told her. "He's in a different place."

"He's moved on," I said empathetically. "You need to move on, too. Your life is different now, and you had no control over what happened to you and Kane."

"It's not that simple," he said huskily. "Those memories… they still haunt me—a lot."

"Maybe you need to replace them with something good," I suggested.

"Like?"

"Like taking me to bed and fucking me until I can't walk tomorrow," I told him as I lifted my head to look into his pain-filled eyes.

A slight smile formed on his lips. "You're a virgin. What do you know about that?"

I rolled my eyes at him. "Just because I've never had sex, doesn't mean I live in a bubble."

Gavin speared his hands into my hair, and bore a hole into my face with his intense gaze. "It's not that I don't want you, Charlie. I think I've wanted to fuck you from the moment we first met. But I'm not the sort of man you need in your life—especially not your first time around. But I will take you to bed. You still look tired."

I squealed as he swung me up into his arms and rose off the couch. He carried me into the dim light of his bedroom, pulled the covers back and plopped me into the middle of his bed.

My breath caught as he stripped down to his boxer briefs, my eyes transfixed by his perfectly sculpted body. Gavin was toned, and I wanted to reach out and trace each delineated muscle with my tongue. He was perfectly, gorgeously made.

He didn't seem to have a single body issue, and he dropped each item of clothing on the floor carelessly until he finally climbed into bed dressed only in his underwear, and then reached out to wrap his arms around me. He covered us both with the sheet and comforter.

My head rested on his shoulder, and I felt safer than I ever had in my entire life.

"Comfortable?" he asked in a deep baritone.

"Yes." I was comfortable, but I could also feel the hard outline of his cock as our bodies melted together.

"Good. Then sleep," he demanded. "I'm not going anywhere. I'll be right here to protect you."

I already knew that. Deep in my soul, I'd always believed Gavin wanted nothing more than to keep me from harm. "Nothing you said tonight makes me feel any differently," I shared in a whisper next to his ear.

"It should," he answered in a coarse voice. "Don't you have any sense of self-preservation?"

"Not with you," I answered as my eyes closed. "I don't need it. You have enough protective instincts for both of us."

"You really don't think of me as an asshole because I was forced to rape my best friend?" There was a certain vulnerability in Gavin's voice that made me try to snuggle closer to him.

"No. Neither of you had any choice, short of ending up dead. You're a survivor, Gavin. I hate what you went through, and I can imagine the guilt you've harbored over the incident. But you need to let it go." There was no way I wanted to see him suffer anymore over something he couldn't control.

He stroked my hair absently as he said, "You never cease to surprise me, Charlie. Most women would have flipped out over my past."

I yawned. "I guess I'm not most women. I can't understand how anybody could blame you for what happened."

"Many would," he replied.

"I still want you. Maybe now more than ever." I wanted to be with Gavin more than I'd ever wanted anything else in my life.

"I want you, too. But it's not going to happen," he answered in a guttural tone as he gave me a playful slap on the ass. "Now go to sleep."

I sighed. "I'm not tired."

"Liar," he scolded.

"I'm still trying to get over the fact that I offered somebody my body for the first time in my life, and he turned me down."

Gavin put his forehead against mine. "I'm not turning you down. Jesus, Charlie, I'd give my right nut to be with you right now. But I can't."

I knew he wasn't lying. I heard the naked desire in his voice. "What happened in the past doesn't matter to me," I argued.

Somehow I sensed that if I couldn't get through to him now, I might never make him understand how I felt. Gavin was a lot like me. He'd continue to be my guardian, but he'd bury his emotions, and I'd never get him to understand the fact that I only cared about the man he was now.

"It fucking matters to me," he growled, then pulled his head back. "You're too damn sweet, too damn innocent for a prick like me."

I broke loose from his hold and straddled his body, wishing I could see his eyes, but the light was too dim, the sun still hours from rising. "I'm not sweet, and I'm far from innocent. Most of the time I walk around wishing I'd died instead of my brother. I feel unwanted, unloved. Just once, I want to feel something more. *You* make me feel something different, something good. Is it so wrong that I want something just for myself for once in my life?" My voice and my body quivered as I stared down at Gavin's face.

He flipped our positions so quickly my head spun, pinning me beneath him so fast I didn't have time to think.

I could hear his ragged breathing as his bulky form towered above me. "Don't say you want to be dead. Don't ever say that," he rumbled. "Talk to me, Charlie... I can't help you if I don't know why you feel that way."

A tear trickled down my face and I shook my head. "No. I just want you."

"I'm no goddamn hero, sweetheart. I'm filth wrapped up in a now successful and legit business. I can't change my past."

"I'm not asking you to," I said emphatically. "I want you exactly the way you are. You're *my* hero, Gavin. You have been since the moment you kept me from dying."

"Fuck! Is there anything I can tell you to change your mind?" he asked desperately.

I knew he wasn't a killer, and he only stole to keep his family fed. "Nope. My opinion stays unchanged. Make me feel good, Gavin. Let me make you understand that the past doesn't matter anymore."

"That's really what you want?" he asked in a low, uneasy tone.

"More than anything. I'm not asking you for anything more. Just now. Just us. Just this." I wrapped my legs around his waist and ground my pussy against his steely erection.

"Then there's no hope for either one of us because I can't fight this anymore," he said in a husky voice as his mouth came crashing down to claim mine.

CHAPTER 19

Charlie

The relief of feeling Gavin's possessive lips on mine, and the nearly palpable sense of him letting go was euphoric. I moaned as our tongues entangled in a scorching embrace, my core flooding with a fiery heat that rose up every time he touched me.

But there was a difference this time.

I knew he was going to satisfy my voracious hunger for him, and finally let go of at least some of his past.

Wrapping my arms around his neck, I had to use my instincts to guess what Gavin wanted. Wanting to be closer to him, I let my palms slide up and down his back, knowing I could never get enough of touching his fiery skin.

"I don't know what to do," I panted as he finally pulled his mouth from mine. "I want to make you feel good, too."

He pulled me gently into a sitting position to slide the pajamas I was wearing over my head. Once he'd tossed them to the floor, he turned on the reading light over the bed so I could see his face. Gavin clasped my hand in his and put our conjoined fingers over his heart.

"You don't have to do a damn thing, Charlie. Do what feels good. Feel this..." He spread my hand over the left side of his smooth, muscular chest. "My heart is racing like I just ran a damn marathon and I've barely touched you. Just knowing you want me makes me crazy."

My own heart flip-flopped as I got lost in his earnest gaze. "I do want you, Gavin. So much," I said breathlessly.

"Feel this..." He moved my hand down to his cock. "You don't have to do a single thing but be near me, for me to want to be inside you."

"Can I touch you?" I asked, desperate to feel him now that I knew he'd end up inside me.

He groaned, but he quickly disposed of his briefs and flopped onto his back. "This is likely to kill me," he complained.

I licked my dry lips as I stared at his enormous erection. Okay, maybe I smiled just a little because of his comment. Intrigued, I reached out and swiped the bead of moisture from the tip of his cock, then licked my finger to see what he tasted like.

"Fuck! Did you have to do that?" Gavin asked in a voice cracking with need.

I looked at him as I sucked on the tip of my finger, savoring the slightly salty flavor of his essence. I reached for him again, tracing a damp finger over the silky head before running my fingers down the long shaft. "I wanted to taste you. Is that bad?"

God, he felt good. He was big, and I knew the first time might be painful, but the wrenching need to have him fill me was a hell of a lot more overwhelming than any possible pinch I might feel from losing my virginity.

"I'm dying here, Charlie," he said coarsely, sounding like his control was sitting on a razor's edge.

I wrapped my fingers around him and stroked up and down. "Tell me what to do," I requested.

"Not. That," he answered through gritted teeth, then rose up and flipped me onto my back.

"That's bad?" I asked as I looked up at him.

"Not usually. But right now, you have me so worked up... I'm not going to fucking last," he answered gruffly. "When you touch me like that, it makes me crazy."

I wanted to ask him what he meant, but before I could get the words out of my mouth, Gavin was kissing me like a man possessed, and I melted into him as my arms wound around his neck.

I whimpered as he pulled his lips from mine, but he put a finger over my mouth. "Easy, baby."

His tongue left a trail of fire down the sensitive skin of my neck as he tasted and teased his way down my body, stopping to linger as he gently sucked on one of my nipples and teased the other with his talented fingers.

I moaned, then speared my fingers through his hair, feeling his touch sizzle through every nerve in my body. "Gavin," I said in a pleading voice.

"You're so damn beautiful, Charlie," he said in a voice muffled by the skin of my belly.

I knew I wasn't a beauty, but Gavin made me feel like I was. The way he touched my body, exploring like he couldn't get enough, made me feel like the sexiest woman in the world.

My core spasmed and clamped down hard as Gavin slipped one of his large hands inside my panties, groaning as he stroked through the moist heat between my thighs.

"You're so damn wet for me, sweetheart," he said in a throaty voice.

My hips rose up to meet his fingers, my body on fire for something more. "Gavin. Please."

One fierce tug and my panties were gone, tossed off the side of the bed. The thought that he didn't have the patience to take them off slowly wound my body tighter with need.

I parted my thighs instinctively, but Gavin put a hand on each of my knees and opened my thighs wider to him before he lowered his head and buried his tongue between my folds, taking one long lick of my pussy from bottom to top.

"Oh, God," I moaned loudly, unable to contain the carnal pleasure that his silky tongue had just fired up in my belly.

I gripped his hair tighter, but nothing prepared me for the erotic, intimate pleasure of Gavin devouring my pussy like he'd been deprived of sustenance for weeks. Lips, teeth and tongue worked together to devastate my senses, my body trembling as he lightly clamped his teeth on my clit.

My head thrashed, my senses still trying to take in the ecstasy of Gavin's mouth all over my pussy, my clit throbbing, begging for more.

"Gavin, I need..." My voice trailed off as I realized that I wasn't exactly certain what I had to have.

"Easy, sweetheart," he said as he lifted his head. "I'll give you what you need. Trust me."

"I do." I squirmed, beneath his touch, knowing that he'd give me that elusive something I had to have. I just hoped he did it before my body imploded.

My hands fisted his hair harder, and I knew I was yanking his locks, but I was helpless to make myself stop.

He explored with his fingers as he teased my clit with his tongue, and I was gulping for breath when I felt his finger impale my sheath. "Yes. Please," I encouraged him, needing to feel him. "More."

I lifted my hips, needing him harder, faster.

"Sweetheart, you're so damn tight," Gavin growled as he eased a second finger inside.

My muscles stretched to accommodate his fingers, my back arching with desperation as he started moving them inside me.

"Gavin," I screamed, feeling the tight coil in my belly start to unfurl and head straight for my core.

He pumped his fingers inside me harder, and his tongue gave me the friction and pressure I needed to finally find release. My entire body shuddered as waves of pleasure like I'd never experienced pounded over my body. Gavin extended my climax, lapping at the juices between my thighs until my chest was heaving and I was gasping for air.

He moved up my body sensually, letting our bodies slide skin-to-skin until he was finally over me, kissing me, and I wrapped my arms around his neck and tasted myself on his lips.

His kiss was short and powerful, but he lifted his head to let me breathe. "Feeling better?" he asked in a husky voice.

I nodded, trying to catch my breath. "I didn't know it could be like that."

Obviously, I'd masturbated in the past. Sometimes I was able to get myself off. But never, ever had I experienced an orgasm that powerful. I didn't even know it was possible.

"I wanted you to feel good, Charlie. It makes me crazy to hear you scream my name," he admitted as he nuzzled my neck.

It wasn't like I couldn't understand what he was saying. But I had the same need. "Fuck me, Gavin. I need you."

Looking up at him with what I knew to be a pleading expression, I saw the muscle in his jaw twitch, our needy gazes colliding as he slowly rose off the bed.

CHAPTER 20

Gavin

"*W*here are you going?" Charlie asked, sounding confused.

Fuck! Fuck! Fuck!

I'd hoped that I'd be able to satisfy myself with just a taste of Charlie, but all it had done was solidify my unrelenting need for her. I fished into the pocket of my discarded pants to pull out a condom. Hell, even before we'd gotten here I'd probably known that I'd find myself in this position.

I was screwed.

I always had been when it came to the beautiful, adorable, innocent woman in my bed. Maybe I'd known that making her mine was inevitable, even when I'd bought a box of condoms on a pit stop when we were coming to the safe house.

"You have condoms?" she asked in a quiet voice. "Do you always have one in your pocket?"

I clenched the package and plopped back onto the bed. Hearing the vulnerability in her voice, I knew it was time to tell her one more truth. Stretching out next to her, I stroked her damp hair, marveling over the fact that this amazing creature actually wanted me. "No, love. I never have them with me these days. I won't bullshit you and tell you that I haven't had my share of women, but I haven't had sex with anybody since what happened with Kane. I couldn't."

She scrunched up her brows in the adorable way she always did when she was thinking. "Why?"

I shrugged. "I couldn't. Every time I thought about sex, it brought up my past, so the two became linked in my mind. As a result, I've avoided sex altogether." But holy fuck...I was making up for lost time with Charlie.

Charlie reached up and grasped my hand and laid it on her chest. "We're different when we're together," she said in a soft, soothing voice. "This is something wonderful for me, Gavin," she confessed.

Looking at the wide-eyed innocent expression on her adorable face, I had to completely agree. I *was* different when I was with her, and my need for her was raw and real. Maybe that intensity pushed aside my guilt and my past.

Releasing her hand, I rolled on the condom, savoring the sensation of my cock pulsating in my hand before I slowly lowered my body over hers, unable to take my eyes away from her adoring gaze.

Charlie wanted me.

She needed me.

But most of all, she accepted me for exactly who I was, and that realization had my chest aching and my heart galloping as I stroked some loose strands of hair away from her face.

Finally, I answered, "This is something incredible for me, too, sweetheart. Maybe it's something I don't deserve, but I don't want to fight it anymore. I need you, too, Charlie. More than you could ever imagine."

This woman was starting to mean everything to me, and I knew as sure as the sun was going to rise that there was no way I'd ever let her go once I had her.

Mine!

"Don't fight it," she insisted. "I've been waiting for you, for this. All my life I've been desperate to feel wanted, even if it was just for a short period of time."

"Baby, I'm always going to want you. Make no mistake about that," I said gruffly as I shifted my body to take her. "There's never going to be another period in your life where you won't be wanted. Not as long as I'm breathing."

I had no idea what kind of number the people in her life had done to Charlie, but it made me fucking insane just to think about her not feeling adored and cherished like she should be.

Her happy sigh made me feel like the most powerful guy in the world, and as I lowered my head to kiss her, I buried myself inside her with one strong stroke, hoping I could quickly move past the painful part.

I inhaled her gasp of surprise as I covered her lips, coaxing them open as I struggled with the desire to pound into her tight little body. And God, she *was* tight. I could feel her muscles stretching to accept me, slick and full to capacity.

Her body was tense, but her arms wrapped tightly around me, and as I stayed still and nipped and licked the sensitive skin of her neck, Charlie relaxed. "You okay, love?" I asked in a husky voice.

"Yeah. I'm okay," she said in a breathless voice.

I peppered kisses on her face, her neck, and her shoulders, waiting for her to give me a sign that she was ready.

It was the longest minute I'd ever experienced.

My cock was throbbing inside her, wedged tightly inside her like it belonged there and always had. My control was dangling by a thin thread, the only thing keeping me from losing it was her innocence and a fear that I'd hurt her.

I let out a breath I hadn't realized I was holding when she hesitantly wrapped her legs around my waist. "More, Gavin. Please."

They were the sweetest words I'd ever heard, and my body, damp with perspiration from holding back, finally shuddered in relief as I pulled back, then buried myself again.

"Yes," she moaned.

That was all I needed to finally let go.

I started as slowly as I could, but I was pounding into her after a few strokes, guided by her body lifting up to meet me, our skin slapping together in our urgent need for each other.

"Mine," I barked, so overwhelmed by the animalistic desire to claim her completely as my own that I couldn't stop the compulsion.

Her nails bit into my back, but I loved the erotic pain. Charlie was claiming me just as surely as I was claiming her.

"Gavin!" Her pleasured scream was sweet, and I shifted to grind into her with every thrust.

"Take what you need, baby," I demanded.

I could feel the pressure at the base of my spine, and I knew I wasn't going to last much longer.

Charlie's sweet body started to undulate against me, and I nipped at her shoulder and her neck, getting lost in the feel of our bodies both straining together to reach one goal.

"Fuck me harder, Gavin."

Her desperate plea made me lose it. I pummeled into her hard and fast, and she pushed up against me, unafraid of taking exactly what she wanted.

My heart was fucking hammering by the time she started to climax, and the clenching, hot flesh of her tight pussy milked me to my own explosive release.

The orgasm rocked me, tilting my whole damn world off-balance as I came with an intensity I'd never experienced before.

"Charlie!" I shouted in a hoarse voice, holding onto her like she was the most precious thing I'd ever had. She was worth hanging onto with everything I had because she actually was the best thing that had ever happened to me.

My chest was still heaving as my world finally tilted upright again, and all that could be heard in the bedroom was the sound of our heavy breathing. I knew I should roll off her, but I couldn't bring myself to let go of her, or disconnect myself from her body while I was trying to recover from something I already knew was a life-changing event for me.

Burying my face into the side of her neck, I willed my heart to slow down, and the emotions I was experiencing to calm. My body eventually responded, but my feelings were still raw. I relished the feel of Charlie stroking her hands over my hair and then my back, wallowed in the sense of not feeling alone for the first time in my life.

"I have to move," I finally told her.

"Why?" she asked as she stretched against me like a happy cat.

Slowly, I disconnected our bodies and rose to my knees to dispose of the used condom, my heart sinking as I saw the smudges of blood on her thighs and the surface of the latex. I rolled off the bed and strode into the bathroom, dumping the condom and bringing back a moist, warm towel.

I wiped the perspiration from her face, and stroked back her damp hair, then used the towel to swipe the blood from her thighs before I placed it against her core.

"I hurt you," I stated flatly. "I'm sorry."

"That feels good, but I could have cleaned up," she protested weakly. "And it only hurt in the beginning. I don't think there's a way to avoid a little bit of pain. But the rest of it was worth it."

Charlie had given me something special and amazing, a precious gift of innocence in a world where I'd known very little except survival. I still didn't quite understand why, but I wasn't going to question something this fantastic.

I stretched out beside her and gathered her into my arms, not even trying to resist the possessive and protective instincts I had for her.

She reached down and tossed the towel to the floor and cuddled up against me.

We fell asleep in a mass of tangled limbs, sleeping hard until we woke up in the exact same position.

CHAPTER 21

Charlie

"Hey, love... what are you up to?" Gavin asked the following morning as he strolled into the living room of the safe house. "And you, Thor... changing loyalties, buddy?" he asked his monster dog as the pup sprawled at my feet with Ripley.

Both dogs rose immediately and attacked Gavin to get their morning dose of affection. He scratched Thor's wiggling body, and rubbed Ripley's body until both canines were satisfied and plopped back down for their nap.

I looked up at him and smiled as he stood back up from his doggie love-fest. "I'm actually working. I'm trying to document what I can remember about the altered virus. I just can't figure out every detail. I thought it might help if the FBI knew exactly what we were dealing with."

Damn, he looked so good in a pair of jeans and a black T-shirt. I shivered as I stared at the powerful body I'd gotten to know so well and so intimately the night before.

Though a few muscles I didn't know I had were burning today, I felt good—and oddly enough, I felt like a different person to who I'd been just a few days ago.

Gavin had changed me.

And I was pretty sure I'd changed him.

After his confession that he hadn't been with anybody in years, I knew my instinct was right about him needing to give in or escape back into his guilt. Kane had obviously moved on, no longer traumatized by what prison had forced on him and Gavin. It was Gavin's turn to let go now.

He plopped down in a chair opposite of my seat on the couch and opened his own laptop that he'd been carrying. "Anything I can do to help?"

"No. Not really. I just thought if I could put the formula together like I saw it that day, it might help. But my exposure was really brief, just long enough to recognize how serious and destructive the research was. Obviously, I didn't know that my boss was making chemical weapons at the time. I thought it was all a big mistake."

Gavin closed his laptop and gave me his total attention. It was one thing I really adored about him. When I was talking or troubled, he listened completely and without distraction. "Was it really bad?"

I nodded. "It was similar to one of the deadliest viruses in the world. I should have thought of it before I went to Doug. There are only a few labs in the entire world that have the facilities to handle any kind of research on viruses that deadly. Our lab didn't handle that class of virus. I guess I was just so concerned that I didn't think before I brought the information to Doug. I should have known something was off."

"You did what any normal person would do, Charlie. This isn't your fault. You got caught up in something that never should have touched you," Gavin grumbled.

"Somebody wants to kill a massive number of people, or at least use that research to hold nations hostage," I mused.

"It won't get that far. I have faith in the FBI team who knows about it now."

"I hope they get to whoever is masterminding this research." I nodded at his laptop. "I guess you were going to try to get some work done."

"Maybe take another look at the dark web," he admitted.

"Will you show me how it all works?" I asked curiously.

"If you want. But it isn't pretty," he warned.

I rolled my eyes. "Which is probably why it's called the *dark* web."

"First, tell me how you're feeling," he insisted.

Gavin had gotten up before I awoke, and we really hadn't had time to talk. By the time I'd showered and brought my laptop out to the living room, it was already late in the morning.

I changed positions on the couch, wincing a little as I moved. "I'm just a little sore."

His sharp eyes assessed me. "More than a little, I think."

I shook my head. "I really am okay."

"A warm bath might help," he suggested.

"Are you planning on joining me?" I teased. The bathtub was enormous, plenty big enough for both of us.

"Don't tempt me until you're not sore anymore," he rumbled.

I knew it might be a while before my muscles weren't aching, but being with Gavin again would be worth a little bit of discomfort. Or maybe it would be worth *a lot* of discomfort.

"I think I'd be lonely in that big tub all alone," I said with false innocence.

"Don't push me, woman," he warned.

I shrugged and twirled the single braid I'd put in my hair after I'd showered. "It was just a thought."

His gorgeous blue eyes turned a darker shade of blue as he seemed to mull the idea over. "Not happening, beautiful. The next time I fuck you, you're going to be pain free."

"It was way worth it," I told him in a husky voice.

"I was wondering if you'd wake up today and come to your senses," he said hesitantly.

I shot him a surprised glance. "What do you mean?"

"After everything I told you last night, I thought you might think about it and realize that you'd given your virginity to a convict who was in no way worthy of you."

"Don't say that!" My tone was sharp and angry. "I hate it when you do that."

Gavin looked taken aback as he stood up straighter in his chair. "Do what?"

I gulped for air to try to form my words. "You piss me off when you put yourself down. Do you realize I've never in my life wanted to be intimate with another guy? Yeah, you're hot and all, but the reason I want to be with you has nothing to do with superficial things. I care about you, Gavin. I admire your tenacity. I love the way you wanted to take care of the rest of your family even when the decks were stacked against you. When it would have been so much easier for you to just give in and join one of the prison gangs, you resisted. You came out of prison and made something out of your life. You help the authorities now instead of running from them. Don't you think all of that means something?"

He shrugged. "I guess it means I'm not a total dick anymore."

I was angry. I didn't get that way often. In fact, I couldn't remember the last time I'd been so pissed off. But if Gavin wasn't going to see for himself who he was now, I was damn well going to show him.

"It means you're a good man, Gavin. Period."

"But what I did to Kane—"

"You had no control over that, Gavin. And Kane's forgiven you," I reminded him. "Give yourself a break. Kane doesn't blame you. Both of you are alive. You're safe. You're successful. Let it go. Please. It hurts me when you put yourself down."

"I'll stop," he answered immediately. "The last thing I want to do is hurt you, Charlie."

I nodded. "Good," I said sharply.

I watched his face as his lips twitched.

"Don't you dare laugh!" I demanded as I pointed a finger at him.

His grin grew broader. "I can't help it, sweetheart. You're so damn adorable when you're mad."

I crossed my arms and glared at him.

"I'm glad to know you still don't have any regrets," he said in a deep, throaty voice.

"I don't."

"Aw, don't be that way, Charlie. I can't help the way I feel sometimes. But I'll try. I swear I will."

My heart melted at his vulnerable admission. "You can't change your past, Gavin, any more than I can change mine. And believe me, I wish I could change a lot of things. The only choice we have is to move on."

"I think I'm moving on," he said with humor in his voice. "Probably because I can feel your foot on my ass."

Maybe I *was* pushing on him, but he needed to go forward.

My own lips started to curve up in a smile. "Believe me, if I could touch that mighty fine butt of yours, it wouldn't be with my foot," I said, loosening up a little.

He rose a wicked brow at me. "Feel free any time."

Now that my anger was dwindling, I felt my face flush. Gavin's willingness to be so obvious about his attraction to me still flummoxed me at times. I wasn't used to having a guy's sexual attention, and I certainly never dreamed I'd have it from a man like Gavin.

"You're so much more than you think you are," I told him earnestly, certain that my heart was probably in my eyes.

"Ditto, Charlie. I'm not the only one who has issues with seeing my worth, sweetness."

He had a point, but... "Our problems are different," I protested. I'd lived most of my life knowing exactly how little I was valued and actually resented by my parents. I wished I could change that, but I couldn't. I turned myself inside out and upside down trying to be what my dad wanted, but someday I had to accept that I'd never be Jessie, and my dad would never forgive me for that.

"I can't help you if you won't tell me what happened, love," he said in a deep, coaxing voice.

My heart ached as I stared across the space between us and into his sympathetic blue eyes. I wanted to tell him. I needed to tell somebody, and Gavin would probably understand. But the old familiar sense of remorse that I'd carried my entire life kept my lips sealed.

I jumped at the distraction of Thor getting up and padding over toward the back door with Ripley right behind him.

"I think they need to go out," I said brightly, avoiding Gavin's assessing gaze as I jumped up to follow the dogs to the door, my heart racing as I thought about spilling out all of my insecurities and my childhood trauma. I'd kept everything locked away for so long, I wasn't even sure I could pull it out again.

I'd done nothing except exist for so long, but now Gavin was starting to wake up parts of me that I'd never even explored.

It felt good.

But it was also frightening.

I opened the door and let the dogs out, watching them from the screen door. Both of them pretty much did their business and then wanted to stay in the yard for a little play time. I smiled at their antics as I watched them chase each other around the yard, both of them blowing off steam.

I cringed as I saw a rabbit duck into the bushes, Thor the first to pick up the bunny's scent.

"No, Thor. Don't you dare," I called out as I opened the screen door to grab him.

Ripley and Thor were both fairly obedient...but they both had a prey drive.

"Dammit!" I cursed as I saw Thor take off into the bush with Ripley right behind.

I raced after the dogs in a pair of jeans and a T-shirt, ignoring the overcast, chilly day in the mountains because of my concern for the dogs, hoping they gave up on the rabbit chase pretty damn quickly.

CHAPTER 22

Gavin

I hauled ass to the door as I heard the muffled cry from Charlie, unsure of what the hell was happening. I got there just in time to see her light blue T-shirt disappear into the bushes, recognizing her calls to dogs as she went.

"Damn dogs," I grumbled, hesitating to grab a loaded 9mm handgun from the kitchen drawer, quickly checking the safety before I tucked it into the small of my back and pulled the T-shirt over it.

I'd been a convict, and I'd also been raised on gang-infested streets. I knew how to handle a gun, and the FBI agents had quietly let me know it was there. If we had to run around chasing dogs, I sure as hell wasn't going without protection for Charlie.

I slammed the door shut behind me, hot on Charlie's trail. The only thing driving me was to find Charlie and my runaway mutts.

I dove into the woods where I'd seen her disappear, realizing there wasn't much of a path, and there were plenty of briars as I pushed through them and finally came out on what looked like a game pathway.

"Charlie!" I bellowed as I followed hers and the dogs' footprints in the dirt.

I hadn't gone far before I came into a clearing, surprised to find a glistening pond right in front of me.

"Nooo! Come back. Please." The pleading voice was Charlie's and it made my blood run cold.

Both of the dogs were in the middle of the damn pond, both of them frolicking in the water. They were bouncing around, their heads occasionally bobbing beneath the water, but it was apparent that neither one of them were in distress.

"Charlie? What the fuck?" I exclaimed with concern.

What in the hell was she doing? She'd waded into the water and was begging the dogs to come back in.

I didn't move fast enough to keep her from diving into what had to be fucking frigid water after the dogs. The pond was no doubt ice-melt, and cold as hell.

"Thor! Ripley! Get your asses here!" I yelled in an angry tone, watching as Charlie's head came up to the surface. "Charlie! What in the hell are you doing?"

The dogs responded immediately, making time to the shore. I waited for Charlie, knowing she'd be right behind them.

I still couldn't figure out what in the hell had possessed her to jump in after them. They were dogs. They could swim. The water was pretty damn cold, but Thor had a heavy coat, and Ripley's was warm enough. I had no doubt both of them would have been headed back to the shore in short order. Neither one of them was going to freeze.

The dogs shook themselves off, then promptly rolled in the dirt, but I wasn't paying much attention to them.

I was too busy watching Charlie.

She wasn't heading back to shore.

She wasn't swimming.

She flailed around in the water, and then a horrified scream left her mouth.

"Fucking hell!" I yanked the weapon from my back and tossed it in the dirt before diving into the freezing water, cursing myself for taking so long to realize something that was now pretty damn clear.

Charlie couldn't swim!!

CHARLIE

I was nine years old again, and my fear was just as terrifying as it had been the first time I'd been swallowed up by frigid water. I tried to gulp for air, but I sucked in the chilly water with oxygen, choking as I tried to keep afloat.

I was so cold, so tired.

When I'd seen the dogs bobbing in the middle of the pond, something in my mind had just snapped.

I'd thought about Jessie and my father.

I'd thought about Thor, Ripley and Gavin. Would Gavin hate me if something happened to Thor?

Just like Jessie, I'd been responsible for Thor and Ripley, and I couldn't watch them drown.

Both incidents melded together until I couldn't focus my mind on what was really happening.

All I knew is that I couldn't breathe, and I was pretty certain I was going to die.

Jessie. I'm so sorry. I'm so sorry I couldn't save you.

My head submerged for what I knew would be the last time. I couldn't stay afloat no matter how much I flapped my arms in desperation.

The rescuing hand that latched onto my braid wasn't gentle. It jerked me to the surface, and a powerful arm wrapped around my shoulders.

"Don't fight me," Gavin's forceful voice demanded in my ear. "Relax."

I still wanted to struggle, but the sound of his voice commanded obedience at the moment, and although I didn't relax as he'd requested, I didn't try to free myself in panic.

It seemed like a long time until we reached shore, but I knew it had only been moments. Gavin lifted me as he gained ground then trudged out of the water bearing all of my wet weight.

I coughed, spewing some water as I fought for breath.

"Breathe, Charlie. Breathe," Gavin coached as he dropped to a patch of grass and rolled me onto my side.

My teeth started to chatter, and my mind was still muddled as I lay there with Gavin, coughing until I could suck in normal breaths again.

"I need to get you warm," he pronounced, then unceremoniously lifted my body up again and starting striding away from the water.

I wrapped my arms around his neck to help him, my entire form shivering from fear and the chill of the air and water.

I relaxed as I saw the muddy dogs following behind us, my confusion clearing.

"Once I make sure you're safe, we're going to fucking talk," Gavin grumbled, tightening his grip on me as he ducked through the bushes and into the yard.

I shook my head, but I knew I was going to tell him everything. I'd acted like a mad woman today, risking his life as well as my own.

He was trying to leave his past behind. Maybe it was long past time that I tried to exorcise my own demons.

I shuddered as he shouldered his way through the door, knowing it would be the hardest thing I've ever done.

CHAPTER 23
Charlie

B y evening, Gavin had made sure I'd seen a doctor. The FBI had discreetly sent somebody to check me over, even though I'd argued with Gavin that I didn't need a physician.

I was also clean, dry, and warm. My brain was functioning normally, and I shook my head wondering what in the hell I'd been thinking when I jumped into the water after the dogs.

In that moment, I'd felt the same panic I'd experienced when Jessie had plunged into the water, and I hadn't thought about anything. I'd just…leapt.

The dogs had been bathed, and were sitting at my feet next to the living room couch, both of them looking at me with sad eyes, like they knew they'd caused some kind of trouble.

Gavin was on the other end of the couch, quiet. We'd eaten and he'd taken away the dishes, insisting that I rest.

Now he was back, and the silence between us was almost deafening.

Finally, he spoke. "I can't make you tell me what in the hell happened today, but I wish you would trust me. You're a brilliant woman. Dogs swim. It was a quiet pond. Neither one of them were going to drown. You obviously *don't* swim, but you dove in after two dogs that were perfectly capable of getting to shore. Why the fuck would you do that, Charlie? Tell me why you'd risk your life like that. The fact that you nearly drowned is killing me."

It was the torment in his voice that made me start talking. "It wasn't exactly the dogs. It kind of was, and I was worried about them, but something happened in my past. Something made me snap. I was confused. I had a flashback, and then the instinct to rescue made me do something really stupid. I'm sorry."

Gavin's body was tense, and I could see him clench his fists on his thighs as he replied, "What happened?"

"I've never talked to anybody about what happened the day Jessie died except when I was nine. I told the police and my parents. That's it."

Gavin nodded, but he didn't speak.

I swallowed the lump in my throat before I started to talk. "Jessie and I were playing outside in the snow when I was nine and he was seven. We had a lake close to our house, but we were forbidden to even get close to the shore. My parents had put me in charge of watching Jessie while we were outside. I was older, and I minded them, so they trusted me, even though I was only nine." I stopped to draw a deep breath and then blow it out, my heart racing as I dug deep inside to where all of the pain was hidden. "Jessie was always a handful. He called me boring because I liked to study, and he said I never wanted to have fun. He ran out onto the ice of the lake. I begged him to come back, but he was a seven-year-old boy who liked to get his way. He didn't listen."

Closing my eyes, I could see the scene in my memory as I continued. I had to fight the urge to slam the door on the images. Breathing raggedly, I kept describing that day. "I was desperate to get him back to shore, but when he wouldn't come back, I finally ventured out onto the ice myself, calling and calling for Jessie to come back. I didn't know what else to do. He turned around to taunt me, but... I think he realized he had gone too far. It was too late. The ice broke and he fell in."

Tears leaked from my closed eyelids, and I gripped the leather couch as I saw the images more vividly. "He was wearing winter clothes. He couldn't get out. The ice kept breaking. Then I heard somebody coming, and I called out to them. I was so happy when I knew somebody was coming to help, but I still had to help Jessie. Time was running out for him. But when I moved closer to him, the ice broke under my own feet."

I wrapped my arms around my body and rocked. "They rescued me. I was closer, and they didn't know Jessie had gone under until it was too late. I let my baby brother die, and it doesn't matter how many times I wished it was me instead of him, he's still gone."

Sobs were wracking my body as Gavin picked me up and cradled me in his arms, rocking me like a child as I wept angry, remorseful, sorrowful tears that I'd never cried when Jessie had died. "My father never let me cry. He said I should be grateful I was alive after I'd let my brother die. My parents hated me, Gavin. My mother hated me until she died, and my father still hates me."

He held me tightly, stroking my hair as he whispered huskily. "No, baby. They couldn't hate you. It wasn't your fault. You were a kid. It was just a horrible accident."

I shook my head, then buried my wet face in his neck. "My father *does* hate me. You have no idea how many times he's told me I should have died instead of Jessie. I know he's right, but—"

"He fucking says that?" Gavin rasped.

"All the time. I've tried my entire life to do something he'd be proud of, but I never have. Jessie would have done better, or he would have been more successful. It doesn't matter what I do. He never lets me forget that I killed my little brother."

"Look at me," Gavin insisted as he moved into a sitting position and pulled me onto his lap.

I kept my face against his T-shirt.

"Charlie, look at me," he rumbled, gently grasping each side of my head to force it back.

Our eyes met, and he locked me into his gaze and wouldn't let go. "You are not responsible for what happened to your brother." He said it emphatically, emphasizing every word. "It was an accident. I don't give a damn what your father says or does. What kind of parent does that shit? Yeah, maybe he was in pain. Maybe deep down inside he couldn't bear to blame himself for not being with you two. But damn him! You're all he's got, and you're the most amazing woman I've ever met. You never should have been blamed for what happened to your brother, and he damn well should have been grateful you were still alive. Fuck knows I am."

"He isn't," I choked out on a sob. "He wishes I'd died, and sometimes I wish that, too. Nobody wants me, Gavin. After Jessie died, nobody cared."

"I. Fucking. Want. You." Gavin's voice was angry, but I wasn't afraid. "Your old man can go to hell. He's done a number on you long enough. You told me I couldn't change my past, Charlie. You can't either. But believe me when I say you're no longer unwanted. You're the best damn thing that's ever happened to me, and seeing you nearly drown today made me realize that if something happened to you, there would be no damn hope for me. There's a reason why you didn't die that day. I fucking need you."

Tears continued to trickle down my face as I saw the fierce intensity in his eyes. "I need you, too," I answered in a tremulous voice.

"Don't do that to me again, Charlie. Don't ever risk your life. I get that you were having a flashback, and it was a knee-jerk reaction. But nothing and nobody is more important to me than you."

Hearing those words from him made my heart ache. How long had I wanted somebody to accept me and want me for who I was? How many times had I wished my brother could still be alive? I was never allowed to grieve his death. But I was doing it now. "I'm so sorry," I whispered as I lifted a hand to stroke along the stubble on his jaw.

"I'm teaching you to swim," he said in a no-nonsense voice.

The thought terrified me, but for Gavin's sake, I'd try. I'd avoided every body of water bigger than a hot tub since Jessie had died.

I nodded hesitantly, letting him know I'd do my best.

"Does it make sense to you now, that your father has completely poisoned your mind when it comes to your brother's death? It's not normal, Charlie. It's sick and twisted."

"It's going to take some time. I've carried the weight of Jessie's death my whole life."

"If I can let go of my past, so can you. It's over, baby."

I sighed. "I missed him. I still miss him. I wonder what he would have been like if he'd lived."

Gavin gently tucked an errant lock of hair behind my ear. "Maybe there would be two geniuses in the family."

I smiled at him, my heart lighter because I could finally talk about my little brother and honor his memory. "I think he would have been an athlete. Maybe some elite quarterback or something? He loved to be outside, and he was already playing sports even when he was seven."

Gavin grinned. "Maybe the athlete idea isn't good. He might have kicked my ass for daring to steal his sister away."

"He could have been so many things, Gavin," I said tearfully.

"I know, sweetheart," he said huskily as his arms tightened around me.

I buried my face in his neck and inhaled his familiar masculine scent, savoring his powerful embrace. He felt warm, comforting, and so very real. "Thank you," I said gently.

"There's nothing to thank me for, Charlie. I think we both need to bury our painful pasts together. We can't change them. But we can move into the future."

"My father—"

"Needs to be taught limits," Gavin said gruffly. "If he can't love you for who you are, and cherish you as a daughter, fuck him. One thing I've learned is that blood isn't always the tightest bond. If he can't treat you like you deserve to be treated, he's baggage you need to dump. Does he know how you feel? Does he realize what he did to you?"

"I don't know," I answered honestly. "I never talked back, and I never argued with him. I felt guilty. I felt responsible. I let him heap anything and everything on my head without ever questioning it. And I never stopped trying to please him."

"It stops now," Gavin demanded.

"You're right," I agreed as I snuggled closer into his warm, hard body.

"Time for bed," Gavin muttered as he rose, hauling my body up with him.

"Stay with me?" I asked hesitantly.

"Was there any question?" he asked with amusement in his voice.

I was already in my pajamas and he placed me gently on the bed before he stripped down to his underwear.

Thor and Ripley trotted hopefully into the bedroom behind us.

I smiled as I watched the two dogs sit beside the bed, Thor's tongue hanging out and his fluffy hair fresh from a bath sticking out everywhere.

"Don't even think about it," Gavin warned the dogs as he slid in beside me and cradled me in his arms.

I saw the hopeful look stay on Thor's face, and my heart melted.

"Maybe just tonight. They just had a bath, and I don't think they understand what happened today."

Gavin rolled his eyes with a pained expression, but he looked over at the dogs and whistled. "Come on, you two. You're lucky Charlie has such a soft heart."

Both pups sprang onto the bed, making it hard to maintain any personal space, but I didn't care. Thor tried to wiggle in between us, but Gavin was having none of that, so Thor flopped over his legs happily, while Ripley got comfortable against my back.

Gavin might act like he puts limits on Thor, but he was a complete marshmallow when it came to both of the dogs. His expression looked pretty content right before he shut off the light, and plunged all of us into darkness.

Holding me tightly in his arms, he snickered as Thor started to snore. "You asked for it," he reminded me.

"I did," I said with a happy sigh.

I fell asleep with every living thing I really cared about on one king-sized bed.

It was the most peaceful sleep I'd had in a very long time.

CHAPTER 24

Gavin

The last few weeks had flown by, and with each passing day, I realized that there could be nothing better than waking up every morning with Charlie in my arms. I still couldn't believe I'd told her everything there was to know about me—and furthermore, I couldn't believe she wasn't fazed by what I'd done, and could somehow see past it all. Yet it would appear that, now that we'd finally gotten brave enough to let one another into our pasts, it was as if we could finally let it go and move beyond it all.

It's not that we didn't still carry the burden of our guilt. We did. She'd never fully forgive herself for her brother's death, just like I'd never fully forgive myself for raping my best friend. Things like that, they left their mark deep on your soul, blackening it with a spot that was impossible to wipe clean. It would always be there, a part of you that you couldn't really escape.

Yet that didn't mean we couldn't move on from the things that haunted us. And now that I had Charlie in my life, it felt like I was getting a second chance, and I'd be damned if I was going to squander this opportunity to finally be happy. But there was more to consider, because I wasn't the only one here.

I had to be better for her.

I had to be the man she deserved—*and then some.*

Because the poor girl had been through enough, and was struggling with demons of her own. She didn't need me pulling her down when I should be the one lifting her up—and I would. I'd do just that, so she'd never spend another day feeling unloved, she'd never spend another day doubting her worth or questioning her existence. I'd lay the moon and the stars at her feet to show her that she meant the world to me.

It didn't matter that I hadn't known her long. She'd quickly become my everything, stealing my heart and making it so I could no longer deny that I was head over heels in love with her.

With her still asleep in my arms, and her naked body nestled against mine, I kissed the top of her head, hoping that she felt how much she was loved, even in her sleep. Her lips curled into a content smile, and then her eyes drifted half open as she started to stir awake, her voice still thick and lazy with sleep. "Morning…"

It'd been nearly two weeks since I first took her to my bed and made her mine—and though I'd given her enough time to heal after our first time together, there'd been no holding me back afterwards. Not now that I had her in my system. She was the blood that pounded through my heart, the air I breathed, and my very sustenance. And the truth was, her sexual appetite was just as voracious as mine, almost as if now that we'd found each other, we were making up for lost time.

"I'm sorry, sweetheart… I didn't mean to wake you." Yet instead of letting her go back to sleep, my hands drifted down the small of her back to her voluptuous ass, cupping her cheeks in my hands as I pulled her to me and caught her mouth in a kiss.

I'd never get my fill of her. And she was all mine.

Yet the moment the dogs realized we were awake, they were desperate to go out.

I groaned, loathe to leave Charlie when she was warm and naked, and far too tempting, though I knew there'd be no stopping the howls of protest if I ignored the pups. "I'll be right back."

"Actually, let me come with you. I wouldn't mind taking a morning hike. I've been feeling a bit cooped up, and the dogs could do with a good run." She hopped out of bed and though she was quickly throwing on some clothes, I couldn't help but stop what I was doing to take her in.

"You're so fucking gorgeous, Charlie... I hope you know that." And she was. She was fucking perfect. There wasn't a single thing I'd change.

"You're biased." She laughed, waving me away as I grabbed her, wrapping my arm around her waist and pulling her to me. "And you're still naked."

"So you noticed." I nipped at her bottom lip and then kissed her, my tongue sweeping over hers in a hunger that would never cease.

Not that the dogs were going to be patient. They knew there'd be no stopping us once we got started, so they voiced their protest until Charlie finally broke our kiss, laughing. "They know us all too well."

"I guess that means I should get dressed." I groaned in protest, but before long, the dogs were running out into the brisk air as we followed behind them, her hand fitting perfectly in mine.

The perimeter was secured, so we'd only get so far, but the area was still large enough to afford us a decent hike. There was something about the fresh mountain air that seemed to calm my soul—which was exactly why I'd bought myself a cabin in the mountains not too unlike the one we were staying in. I didn't stay there as often as I liked, but knowing how much Charlie enjoyed this cabin, I couldn't wait to take her to my place and snuggle up in front of a fire with her in my arms.

But first, we needed to sort out this mess with the virus. I hated that her life may still be in jeopardy, and not a moment went by that I didn't worry about her.

"I swear, it's so peaceful up here… it's so easy to forget that someone wants me dead. I'm going to miss this place when it's time to go." When Charlie let out a weary sigh, I stopped walking and pulled her into my arms.

"This will all be over soon, love. And then… we can get on with our lives. *Together*." There was no way I was letting her go. I couldn't, even if I wanted to. She'd quickly become an integral part of my life, and I needed her more than I needed the air I breathed.

"You really mean that?" I couldn't believe she looked surprised.

"Sweetness… I clearly haven't done a good enough job in showing you just what you mean to me. Because if you think this thing between us is coming to an end as soon as you're safe, you can guess again. There's no way in hell I'm letting you go." My words were but a growl as I cupped her face and ran my thumb over her plump ruby red lips. Unable to resist her, I stole a kiss that left me tempted to throw her over my shoulder and haul her back to bed so I could ravish her thoroughly. My tongue clashed with hers, our kiss deepening, so that by the time we managed to come up for air, my head was spinning and my heart was hammering inside my chest. With my eyes locked on hers, I spoke the words that now marked my soul. "I love you, Charlie… I think I've loved you from the moment I first laid eyes on you."

"I love you too, Gavin. I still can't believe I'm lucky enough to have you in my life." She threw her arms around my neck and held onto me as I buried my face in the crook of her neck, holding her tightly to me.

"I'm the lucky one, love." *The luckiest man alive now that I had Charlie in my life.*

We walked hand in hand back towards the house when my phone started buzzing—and given that no one but the FBI had this number, it wasn't a call I was willing to ignore. A shot of adrenaline sent my pulse racing as I pulled Charlie to a stop and dug out my phone.

"Hey... Tell me you have good news, Lou." 'Cause if he didn't, then I knew the alternative reason for his call likely wasn't any good.

The tone of Lou's voice immediately told me we were in trouble. "I'm sorry, Gavin. I've got my men on their way to move you and Charlie to another location. They'll explain everything once it's safe to do so. Our suspect is in the wind, and if your position's been compromised, then I don't want to take any risks."

"Fuck. We'll be ready in five." I was already pulling Charlie towards the house, motioning with a tilt of my head to let her know that we had to get going. I hung up just as we walked into the cabin and headed straight for the bedroom so we could grab our things. "They're moving us to a new location."

She looked stunned. "Where?"

"I don't know, love. But they'll keep us safe. *I'll* keep you safe." I quickly stuffed whatever we had into a duffle bag. I hated that Charlie looked so scared, and though we had little time to spare, I took a moment to pull her into my arms and hold her to me. "I swear it'll be okay, love. I don't want you worrying about anything."

She nodded, trying to put on a brave face, though it was clear she was still shaken up. "I know you'll protect me. I just still can't believe this is happening."

It'd been easy to forget the sort of trouble she was in when we'd been safely cocooned in each other's arms, tucked away in a warm and cozy cabin, high in the mountains. But the danger was all too real—and getting all the more real with each passing moment.

The knock on the door sent Charlie jumping into my arms in a panic. I kissed the top of her head. "I need you to stay here—the dogs will keep you safe. It's likely just our FBI detail coming to move us. But if you hear anything out of the norm, head into the woods."

"I'm not leaving without you, Gavin. *I can't.*" She grabbed my arm, her eyes wide with fear.

"Nothing's going to keep me from you, sweetheart. But I need to get the door before they bust it down." I hated having to let her go, but the pounding was getting louder. Luckily, she nodded and took a step back as I shifted my focus, my mind and body automatically going into survival mode, hating that I didn't have my surveillance equipment.

I grabbed the gun from the nightstand, quickly checked it, and headed to the door, relieved to see Beck and Weston, our current FBI detail. I let them in before locking up behind them. "Lou called. What the hell happened?"

"We need to go." Weston wasn't exactly talkative, though I couldn't blame him. "Are you ready?"

"Yeah... let me get Charlie." The moment she spotted me, she leapt into my arms, and fucking hell, it felt good to hold her. "It's okay, love. They're just moving us as a precaution."

I grabbed our bags, hefting them over my shoulder before grabbing her hand, needing her to know that I was right there by her side, and she wasn't alone in all this. We were ushered into the back seat as the dogs were put into the back of the massive bullet-proof SUV, and then moments later we were rushing down the road with Charlie tucked in at my side.

"What the hell happened?" I needed to know just how big the threat was. Was the threat imminent or was this really just a precaution?

Beck shook his head, looking more frustrated than worried. "We caught the hitman. Set up a decoy of Charlie to trap him— and it worked, too. Got him to flip on his boss—Khasanov, a

Chechen operative with deep pockets and ties to several terrorist groups. He's been stateside, conducting business, so we issued a warrant for his arrest. But... he managed to slip through our net, and now he's in the wind. We're not sure if he knows Charlie's location, and chances are good he won't bother to come after her when we're breathing down his neck. But we're not taking any chances. Honestly, this move is just a precaution on the off chance he decides to try anything."

I was relieved that this was more of a precaution than an outright threat. And hopefully it meant this nightmare would soon be over for Charlie. "If you already have the hitman and he's willing to talk, then that means you have two people who can testify against this guy... Khasanov. Right? Does that mean that they're less likely to come after Charlie?"

Beck shrugged, shifting in his seat to face us. "We hope so. There's a good chance that Khasanov will just try to get out of the country and head back to his home country. At this point, it wouldn't surprise me if he decided that he's better off cutting his losses here. But I'm not sure we'll find him before he leaves the country, since I doubt he's been hanging around, waiting for us to find him."

"But what about the virus?" Charlie shook her head, anger in her eyes. "There's so much unrest in that part of the world. He'll either use the virus to further his own causes, or sell it to the highest bidder, right? We can't let that happen. The virus will kill indiscriminately. Women, children, innocent people... *they'll all die.*"

I tightened my hold on her, hating to see her upset, though trying to right all the wrongs in the world felt like an impossible task. "Unfortunately, some people don't think past lining their pockets, even if it means they're doing so with the blood of innocent people. But you stopped him, Charlie. Chances are good they never got to finish their plans for the virus because you spoke up when you realized that something was wrong. You now have him on the run."

She shook her head no. "I was just doing my job, Gavin. You're the one who's gone well out of your way to save people."

"Sweetheart, you're the one who saved me."

CHAPTER 25

Charlie

*T*his day had barely started and it already felt like I'd been hit by a whirlwind, my emotions a mixed bag of fear and happiness. I was in love with the most amazing man, and I knew that Gavin didn't take that sort of thing lightly. If he said he loved me, then he meant it. And if he said we would be together once this was all over, then I knew that's exactly what would happen.

All we had to do was survive long enough to make it happen.

Though I knew we were a long way from being safe, I held onto what little hope I had, knowing that the FBI were doing all they could, and Gavin would never let me come to harm.

Still not sure of where the agents were taking us, I snuggled up against Gavin's side as he held me tightly to him, knowing that if I had him in my corner, I could deal with whatever there was to come. In less than two weeks, he had managed to erase a lifetime of hurt and guilt, replacing it with nothing but love, understanding, and acceptance.

It's not that I didn't still feel guilty about losing my brother that day so many years ago. But I now knew that it wasn't my fault.

Bad things sometimes happened—and no one was to blame.

I had promised Gavin that I would have a heart-to-heart with my father, and tell him how I felt. I couldn't have a healthy relationship with him if he continued to blame me for my brother's death. And though I didn't hold out much hope for our relationship changing, at the very least I would know that I had tried. And if he couldn't see me for the person I was, the person I'd become, and if he couldn't see the truth about what happened that day, then maybe I was better off without him in my life.

It was hard coming to that realization, but it had become clear that even though he was my father, my own flesh and blood, I may be better off without him in my life. *And I hated that.* He was the only family I had left, but the reality was I couldn't continue to have him in my life if he was going to do nothing but berate and belittle me into feeling guilty for a death I had no control over.

I was never going to be my brother.

No one could replace him.

And I didn't want to try to take his place.

But that didn't mean that my life held no value. And if my father couldn't see that, then it was his loss. It had taken Gavin storming into my life to make me see that I was worth something, and I'd be damned if I was going to let *anyone* drag me down again — let alone my father, who should love me unconditionally.

The impact of a car crashing into us whipped my body against my seatbelt, my head snapping to the side as it collided with something hard, the pain of the impact splintering through my temple as darkness engulfed me. I tried to hold on to the sliver of consciousness that kept wanting to escape me — and then I heard Gavin's voice... Felt his arms holding me against him as I forced my eyes to open.

"Gavin..." My own voice sounded distant to my own ears as I struggled to clear my head and wrangle my thoughts through the ringing in my head and the barking dogs.

"It's okay, love… I've got you. You're safe." It was clear by the way he was holding me, that he was trying to shield my body with his. Always keeping me safe, even if it meant putting his life on the line.

And then I heard it… The rapid and deafening sound of gunshots that easily outran the pounding of my heart.

My mind raced through a million thoughts in that split second—Gavin, the agents, the dogs… If any of them got hurt, it would be because of me. It was my fault that we were in this mess, and I'd never forgive myself if anything happened to any of them.

My father's voice mocked me… telling me that I'd be the end of everyone around me… that they'd pay the price simply for being in my presence.

Except that I was no longer the little girl he could belittle, and despite the chaos surrounding me, I pushed his voice out of my head, once and for all.

We were flying down the road as the agents quickly relayed information to their headquarters, requesting immediate backup as they tried to maneuver us to safety. I held onto Gavin, nestling deep into the safety of his arms as he told me over and over that everything would be okay, even as the other vehicle rammed us again, from the rear this time, the hard jolt only slowing us down momentarily.

I focused on Gavin's words, as he told me everything would be okay. And despite everything… despite the attack… despite the gun fire… I believed him as he held me tightly to his muscular body, shielding me from harm.

We raced around the winding mountain roads, each second feeling like an eternity as time ticked by and we got rammed again and again.

Finally, I heard sirens breaking through the roar of our vehicle's revving engine. I didn't know how long it had been when we finally pulled to a stop, but I swore it'd be another week before I got my heart to slow back down to a normal rhythm.

Beck and Weston exited the vehicle, guns drawn and shouting out orders, as Gavin cupped my face in both his hands, his bright blue eyes locking on mine, even as chaos broke out all around us. "Tell me you're okay, Charlie."

I nodded that I was fine. "Is it over? Is everyone okay?"

"Everyone's fine, love. And it'll be over soon. Real soon."

Luckily, Gavin was right. It was at least another fifteen minutes before we were told that we were in the clear, and it was all over, with Weston giving us the update. "We got him. We got Khasanov."

"Does that mean I'm in the clear? That no one else is going to try and come after me?" I didn't want to get my hopes up just to have them dashed, yet it was hard not to be hopeful.

Weston gave me a smile—the first one I'd seen from him—a wave of relief washing over me. "It's all over. Once we knew who we were dealing with, we got a warrant to search Khasanov's properties and accounts. We were able to track down enough evidence to lock him away for a very long time, even without your testimony. He could still come after you, but it'd be damn hard for him to manage it, and it wouldn't accomplish a single thing since we have him on all sorts of other crimes that go well beyond him trying to make a weaponized virus."

I let out a huge breath that I hadn't even realized I was holding in. "I can't believe it's finally over."

"Now you can get back to your life." Beck gave me a smile, and though I smiled back, his words left me just a little shaken. "We'll be back in just a few. Need to wrap things up here."

I nodded, managing a smile that I knew wasn't fooling anyone. It's not that I wasn't happy to finally be safe, but… *getting back to my life?* My life before this all happened was pretty miserable outside of work. And I didn't want a life without Gavin in it.

Though I wanted the freedom to come and go as I pleased without worrying about someone putting a bullet in my skull, I didn't want to go back to the life I'd been living. I wanted my current reality, where I got to wake up in Gavin's arms every morning—just without killers and weaponized viruses.

Gavin pulled me into his embrace, his head bent to mine. "Hey, love... what has you looking so bothered?"

"Going back to my old life... It's not that I didn't have a decent life and a job I loved. But... I was pretty lonely, Gavin." The rest of my words stuck in my throat, not wanting to speak them and give them power, as if they might become a reality.

"You'll never be lonely again, Charlie. We may be going back to our lives, but our lives are now together, forever linked. Because I'm not letting you go. I don't care if we live in your place or mine—or if we get a new place altogether, and start from scratch with a place that holds no history for either of us. But, no matter what we decide—*we're going to be together.*" He spoke the words with such an intensity, I couldn't help but believe him. "I meant it when I said that I love you. Nothing will ever change that."

"I love you too. More than anything."

Just a week later, and Gavin had scheduled the movers to haul all my things over to his home, after we'd decided that his place was a hell of a lot bigger than mine, and far more secure. It's not that there was any threat now that Khasanov was in custody, facing charges for a countless number of crimes. But better safe than sorry, and the one thing I'd learned was that Gavin did *not* take chances when it came to me.

I still couldn't believe how much my life had changed in just a month's time. But it had. In every way possible—and most certainly for the better.

Gavin was *perfect*. I knew he had a past and his demons would never fully release him, but I'd never met a better man, and *no one* had *ever* cared for me more. Which was pretty damn sad when my parents were included in that list.

I was doing my best to try and get past all that, and with Gavin's help, I was doing so much better. But... it was hard when I knew my father was still out there blaming me for my brother's death. I had finally accepted the fact that it hadn't been my fault. I had been a kid—and a young one at that. And I'd done all I could to try to save Jessie.

Not that my father saw it that way.

"Hey... you okay?" Gavin cupped the back of my neck and pulled me to him, wrapping his strong arms around me. "I know moving can be overwhelming, but the movers will take care of everything. You don't need to worry about a thing. And if you'd rather not live here, we can go anywhere you'd like. Maybe a cabin in the woods?"

I shook my head no. "It's not that. And though a cozy cabin in the mountains would be nice, your place is incredible. And I'm honestly not all that attached to most of my stuff. It's all good as long as I have you and the pups."

"Then what's stolen your smile away?" His eyes darkened with concern as he held me to him.

"I keep thinking of my dad. I know I should just let it go, since nothing's going to change his mind about what happened. But... he's the only family I have left, and it really bothers me that he blames me for something that wasn't my fault." Now that I'd come to terms with what happened that day, I realized that the way my parents had treated me wasn't just wrong, it was horrible. Because instead of losing just their son that day, they'd lost their daughter too—except that the blame for *that* rested solely on their shoulders.

No one else's.

"Maybe you should talk to him, Charlie. I know it won't be easy, but it might be the only way to move past this and lay it to rest once and for all. At the very least you'll know where you stand so you can move on with your life. Because I'm going to tell you right now that if your father can't see the truth of what happened and how he's treated you, I'm not going to let him continue to treat you like crap." When he kissed me, he calmed my soul and chased away my worries. "If you'll let me, I'll be all the family you'll ever need, love."

His words had my heart racing. "You're all I'll need and so much more, Gavin. But maybe you're right. Maybe I do need to speak to him."

"Then no matter what happens with your father, know that I'll be by your side." He linked his hand with mine, and his mere touch was enough to calm me.

In the end, I didn't have it in me to speak to my father face-to-face. Maybe I was being a coward, but I knew it'd be easier to get it all out if I didn't have to do it in person, and as it were, I would still have to muster all the courage I could just to get the words out.

Gavin sat by my side and held my hand as I made the call. "Daddy?"

"Charlie," he grumbled, sounding annoyed, as if I had interrupted his busy day, when I knew damn well he was likely doing nothing more than watching TV and drinking beer. "What is it?"

Gavin stiffened at my side, and I was thinking that if we'd made the trip in person, it'd have taken Gavin all he had not to have some serious words with my father.

I took a deep breath, steeling myself to get the words out that I'd rehearsed in my head a million times over. "It wasn't my fault, Daddy. I need you to know that. I did all I could to save

Jessie—and nearly lost my life in the process. And I know you've blamed me. But I'm calling to let you know that you either need to come to terms with what actually happened that day, or... Or I can't be in your life anymore. I refuse to be your punching bag."

"What the hell are you talking about, girl? How dare you talk to me that way! You were the only one there—and your brother was your responsibility. You *never* should have let him go on the ice."

"As if I could have stopped him? I was nine, Dad. *Nine!* And you know damn well that he *never* listened to me. He was too much of a handful for even Mom to deal with, so how the hell was I supposed to keep him under control?" It was nothing but the truth. I loved Jessie, but it didn't mean he didn't get himself in more than his fair share of trouble.

"Don't you dare speak to me that way. You were the one who was supposed to be watching him."

"That's where you're mistaken. He wasn't my responsibility—*he was yours.* Maybe if you'd taken more of an interest in him instead of watching TV and drinking beer, then you'd have been there to keep an eye on him, and he'd still be alive." My tears streamed down my cheeks, but I didn't care. I'd held all of this in for years, and needed to get it out. "You made your choice. And you didn't just lose him that day—you lost me too. I'm done feeling guilty about something that was nothing more than a tragedy—and I'm done with letting you use me as a punching bag for your own guilt. I'm done, Daddy. I love you, but... *I'm done.*"

CHAPTER 26

Gavin

Fucking bastard. It'd been days since Charlie spoke to her father, and yet her mood had yet to improve. She'd said she was glad she'd finally confronted her father and said her piece so that she could stop carrying around a burden that hadn't been hers to bear, but it didn't mean it had been easy for her. Especially when the jerks she worked for had let her go when she'd dropped off the face of the earth several weeks ago with no clear indication as to when she'd be back.

I had wanted to hold off on my plans, wanting to make sure everything was perfect. Except that none of that mattered now. Not when I needed her to know that no matter what happened with her dad, I'd be right there by her side. "Come on, love. We're going on a bit of a road trip. There's a place I want you to see, and we've been cooped up for too long."

She groaned, though she didn't protest, when I grabbed her hand and led her towards the front door. "What about the dogs?"

"Sweetness... do you really think I'd leave them here? They're coming with us, of course." I whistled to them, and before long, we were all cruising down the highway. I reached over and grabbed her hand, bringing it to my lips, even as I focused on the road ahead. "I was thinking... maybe instead of getting another job, you could do something you've always wanted to do."

She pouted, shaking her head no. "I need to have a job, Gavin. I know we're living together—and I get that you have plenty of money. But I'm not going to just mooch off you and not pay my way."

I loved her independence and sense of fairness. She really was perfect—and she was all mine. "What if I told you that I wanted to start a program to help underprivileged kids get a head start in tech and science, and I want you to run it?"

"*What?*" She shifted in her seat to face me, and I couldn't help but toss her a smile before focusing back on the road. "That would be amazing, Gavin. But..."

"But nothing, sweetheart. Unless you wouldn't be interested in putting that sort of program together." Yet I already knew she'd love nothing more than to help kids achieve things they might not otherwise get the opportunity or access to. "We could even name it after your brother, if you wanted."

With tears shimmering in her eyes, she threw her arms around my neck and kissed my cheek, making me wish I wasn't driving at the moment. "I can't believe you'd do that for me."

"Sweetness, I'd give you the moon and the stars if I could." It was nothing but the truth. "Anything to make you happy."

"I don't need anything but you to make me happy, Gavin. But *this*... the lives you could change with this sort of program... *It'd be incredible.*" Whatever darkness had been haunting her these last few days was suddenly wiped clean by her excitement—and I was loving every minute of it.

We spent the rest of the car ride tossing around ideas for the program, as she enthusiastically jotted down notes in a little notebook she always kept in her purse. She even came up with a name, taking my suggestion to name it after her brother.

Jessie's Second Chance STEM Initiative.

I fucking loved her so much—and it healed my very soul to see her so happy.

As caught up as she was with her plans, it caught Charlie by surprise when we pulled down the driveway that led to my mountain home. I loved the peace and quiet up here in the woods, even if it had been woefully underused.

And now, I was now hoping to change all that.

"Where are we?" Charlie looked out the window, craning her neck to see past the massive oaks and conifers to catch a glimpse of the surrounding mountains, and the log cabin that peeked from behind the trees.

"I'm hoping that you'll consider making this our new home." I slid the car in park just in time to catch her as she threw her arms around my neck and kissed me, our tongues clashing for a heated moment before I forced myself to pull away. "Come on, love. I can't wait for you to see the inside. I think you'll really like it."

"How could I not? The views are breathtaking. And the cabin is adorable." When she smiled at me, I couldn't help but steal a quick kiss before jogging around the car to get her door and help her down from my SUV.

With the dogs out of the back and exploring their newfound territory, I led Charlie up the stairs of the massive front porch, and into what I'd hoped would be our new home. I heard her breath catch as we stepped inside. "Come on... you have to see the view off the great room."

"Gavin... *the fireplace!* It's gorgeous—and *huge.*" Tumbled river stone was stacked up to the ceiling, and the fireplace was probably a good twelve feet wide, with a thick, rough-hewn, wood mantle adding the crowning touch. And then she gasped, as her gaze turned to the wall of glass and the deck just beyond. "I swear... I don't think I've ever seen a more amazing view."

"It was built with the view in mind. Nothing's better than sitting out on the deck with a cup of coffee and watching the sun rise." I pulled open the French doors so she could step outside and get an unobstructed view of the mountains and the forest as they sprawled out before us.

But I had something else to show her.

And when she turned around, it was to find me down on one knee, holding out the engagement ring I'd bought her.

"Charlie... I can't find the words to tell you just what you mean to me. But from the moment you walked into my life, you've changed my world around for the better, and I couldn't imagine spending a single day without waking up to you in my arms. I love you, Charlie Wenham... Would you do me the honor of marrying me?"

CHAPTER 27

Charlie

I gasped when I first saw Gavin down on one knee. It was the last thing I'd expected—and yet it couldn't have been any more perfect, my heart overjoyed with happiness. "I'd love nothing more, Gavin. I love you so much."

He slipped the most beautiful diamond ring onto my finger, and then held onto me as I jumped into his strong arms and kissed him, while he spun me around until I was laughing. "You've made me one hell of a happy man, sweetness."

I covered his face in kisses, as tears of joy slipped down my cheeks. "I swear, Gavin… until I met you, I don't think I realized that I was *still* drowning. But… *you saved me*."

"Then we saved each other, Charlie. Because it wasn't until you walked into my life that I finally felt like I could breathe again." With my feet back on the ground, he cupped my face in his hands and kissed me, sweetly at first, but as one kiss led to the next, there was no holding back for either of us.

With his hands trailing down my back to my ass, Gavin lifted me up off my feet, my legs wrapping around his waist as he carried me inside and straight to a bedroom I'd yet to see. Not that I could be bothered to look at the space when our kisses deepened, his tongue clashing with mine, as our clothes were quickly shed, landing haphazardly in a heap on the floor.

"Please, Gavin... I need you so bad." My words were spoken in a groan of desperation, my lips still pressed to his, as I reached down between us, stroking his long, hard cock. He laid me back against the pillows, lowering his muscular body to mine, his cock teasing me as it slipped through my slick folds.

When my legs tightened around his thighs to pull me to him, he groaned and stiffened. "Condom, baby girl..."

"Or..." I was desperate to have him take me skin to skin... desperate to have him stretch me tight with nothing between us... and I was desperate to have him fill me with his seed, especially now that we were engaged. "Unless you don't want to."

His answer came in the form of a needy grunt as he took me bare, burying his massive cock deep inside me with a single thrust. "Fucking hell, Charlie... it's all I've been able to think about. You feel so good... and I love you so much."

Before I could tell him just how much he meant to me, his mouth was catching mine in a hungry kiss, his tongue clashing with mine, as he started to take me hard and fast. It was as if he couldn't hold himself back, and I may not have been with anyone before Gavin, but I reveled in the intensity with which he took me. It was as if our coming together joined us both body and soul, marking me as his, just as I marked him as mine, knowing there could be no one else for either one of us.

It was almost as if fate had brought us together.

Overwhelmed by it all, and yet wanting more, I raked my nails down his back to spur him on, his pace quickening until he was pounding each thrust into me, so that I felt him down to the marrow of my bones. Gavin already had me teetering on the edge of coming, when he flipped our positions, so that I was now straddling him, his cock still buried deep inside me.

"*Gavin...*" I could barely hold back my orgasm as I rocked my hips up and down his length. But when he sat up and wrapped his arm around my waist and sucked my nipple into his mouth, my orgasm hit me like a bolt of lightning.

"That's it, sweetheart... come for me." His voice was gruff and hoarse with his own need, as I cried out, riding out the waves of pleasure that washed over me, his mouth catching mine in a hungry kiss. Yet he didn't miss a beat, continuing to thrust up into me and drawing out my orgasm until he too was coming, his cock pulsing deep inside me, filling me with his hot seed as he covered my face in kisses. "I can't wait to make you my wife, Charlie... I want a family... kids and dogs everywhere... and nothing but joy and happiness."

"I can't imagine anything more perfect." And I truly meant it. "I love you, Gavin."

"I love you too, Charlie."

EPILOGUE

Charlie

SIX MONTHS LATER...

I couldn't believe I was actually getting married.

I stood back in the hallway as everyone took their places, feeling like a princess in my long white dress and a gorgeous bouquet of flowers that Anna had helped me pick out.

Kane and Anna had been like the family I'd never even hoped to find. Kane's wife was so much like me. She'd become a hermit herself, disconnected from the world while she was struggling with her own loss issues before Kane had come into her life in the most unexpected of situations.

Anna winked at me as she started down the aisle, having agreed to be my maid of honor. I smiled back at her, a happy, radiant smile that I couldn't suppress because I knew that in a matter of minutes, Gavin would be my husband.

Finally, in her own beautiful teal gown, Anna headed down the aisle before me.

"Are you ready, Charlie?" my father's voice grumbled beside me.

I turned my head to look at him, then smiled as I noticed the twinkle of something almost like pride in his eyes.

The road to a truce had been rocky with my dad. Maybe we'd never have a truly close father/daughter relationship, but we were learning to be friends. He'd manned up to the fact that I never should have been held responsible for Jessie's death, and he'd treated me with courtesy. Gavin wouldn't allow him to communicate with me in any other way. Maybe we'd grow closer in time, but I was content to have him here today. He was my only family, and it seemed only right that he was here to give me away.

I finally nodded at him. "More than ready."

"He seems like a decent man," my father said grudgingly.

Really, what more could he say? Gavin was wealthy, brilliant, and he'd been responsible for starting a worthwhile charity that honored my father's deceased son.

"He's perfect," I whispered as I took the arm my dad offered. "You're looking very smart today."

My escort was dressed in a stunningly handsome suit, and was more formal than I'd ever seen him in my entire life.

"I only have one daughter to give away. It seemed appropriate," he replied, bemused.

I leaned up on my tiptoes and kissed his cheek. It was the closest I'd gotten to him since I was a child.

"He better take good care of you," he said, looking flustered by a show of affection from his daughter.

There were no worries there. Gavin cherished me and watched out for me better than any other person ever had.

Even Gavin's brother and sister had taken me under their wing, so happy that Gavin was finally settling down, and I knew neither one of them wanted anything to ruin their eldest sibling's new attitude and joy.

"He will," I murmured to my father as I stepped forward with him to take our place at the end of the aisle.

I looked out over the sea of people in the venue, still a little startled by how many had showed up for what had started out as a very small, intimate wedding.

Everyone stood, and in the front rows, I could see Gavin's brother and sister right next to Kane's brothers. Other than that, many of the people were strangers except for a few of my friends sprinkled throughout the gathering.

Gavin swore most of the people coming to our nuptials were just work associates, but I knew that in some way or another, Gavin had touched many of their lives. I noticed that even a few FBI officers were present.

My husband-to-be was oblivious to just how much his work on disassembling the dark net had endeared him to so many.

My father urged me forward and I went willingly, my heart surging as I heard the start of the wedding march.

When my gaze finally landed on the end of the aisle, I first smiled at Kane, who was looking incredibly handsome in his tuxedo. He was standing next to Gavin, grinning mischievously as I made my way to them.

Anna was waiting for me so she could take my bouquet.

And Gavin? Well, he looked good enough to devour. Our eyes locked, and he wasn't smiling. His look was hungry and predatory, a fact that didn't faze me in the slightest. It was an expression I was accustomed to, and it made a shiver of excitement slither down my spine.

My father made the exchange from his possession to Gavin's, and only then did my groom grin at me. Anna took my bouquet, and I faced my soon-to-be husband with a silly smile that I couldn't wipe off my face.

"I love you," I blurted, unable to hold the words inside me for another second.

His grin grew wider. "I love you, too, baby. You look beautiful."

The Justice of the Peace protested that Gavin was jumping the gun as he leaned down and kissed me with a tender promise of everlasting devotion, taking his time even though the JP was clearing his throat with irritation.

I snickered as he finally pulled back, then nodded to the JP. "We're ready. We were just practicing."

"Looks like you already know that part just fine," the official replied, then started the ceremony.

Gavin winked at me, then squeezed my fingers, showing not the least bit of hesitation or fear. My heart was lodged in my throat as I repeated my vows, still incredulous as to how I'd ended up with a guy like the one in front of me, promising me his trust and love for the rest of our lives.

Then, I reminded myself that I'd waited a long time for him, and those lonely years had paid off big time.

The science geek had gotten her perfect computer geek, and it was only right that the two of them should live happily ever after with each other.

And that's exactly what we did.

~ *The End* ~

ABOUT THE AUTHORS

J.S. SCOTT is a NY Times & USA Today bestselling author of erotic romance. She's an avid reader of all types of books and literature. Writing what she loves to read, J.S. Scott writes both contemporary erotic romance stories and paranormal romance erotics. They almost always feature an Alpha Male and have a happily ever after because she just can't seem to write them any other way! She lives with her husband in the picturesque Colorado Rockies.

Please visit me at:
Website http://www.authorjsscott.com
Facebook https://www.facebook.com/authorjsscott
Twitter https://twitter.com/AuthorJSScott

You can write to me at mailto:jsscott_author@hotmail.com

Subscribe to my newsletter and receive three never before published short stories.

CALI MACKAY is a New York Times and USA Today bestselling author. She lives in New England with her husband, two girls, their crazy mutt and two mischievous cats. When not tapping away on her laptop and getting her characters into trouble, she can be found designing book covers, wrangling her girls, and splicing DNA.

She's also a decent potter, adventurous cook, and horrible gardener. For more information, please go to http://calimackay.com.

BOOKS BY J.S. SCOTT

Billionaire Obsession Series

The Billionaire's Obsession (Simon & Kara)
Heart of the Billionaire (Sam & Maddie)
The Billionaire's Salvation (Max & Mia)
The Billionaire's Game (Kade & Asha)
Billionaire Undone (Travis & Ally)
Billionaire Unmasked (Jason & Hope)
Mine for Christmas (Simon and Kara Short Novella)
Billionaire Untamed (Tate and Lara)
Billionaire Unbound (Gabe and Chloe)
Billionaire Undaunted (Zane and Ellie)
Billionaire Unknown (Blake and Harper)
Billionaire Unveiled (Marcus Colter) (Coming July 25, 2017)

Sinclair Series

The Billionaire's Christmas (Grady Novella)
No Ordinary Billionaire (Dante)
The Forbidden Billionaire (Jared)
The Billionaire's Touch (Evan)
The Billionaire's Voice (Micah)
The Billionaire Takes All (Julian)
The Billionaire's Secret (Xander) (Coming November 7, 2017)

Walker Brothers Series

Release (Trace)
Player (Sebastian)
Dane (TBA)

A Dark Horse Novel

Bound
Hacked

Taken By A Trillionaire Series

Taken By a Trillionaire
Virgin for the Trillionaire by Ruth Cardello
Virgin for the Prince by J.S. Scott (Coming June 6, 2017)
Virgin to Conquer by Melody Anne (Coming July 3, 2017)

The Sentinel Demons

The Sentinel Demons: The Complete Collection
A Dangerous Bargain
A Dangerous Hunger
A Dangerous Fury
A Dangerous Demon King

The Vampire Coalition Series

The Vampire Coalition: The Complete Collection
The Rough Mating of a Vampire (Prelude)
Ethan's Mate
Rory's Mate
Nathan's Mate
Liam's Mate
Daric's Mate

Changeling Encounters Series

Changeling Encounters: The Complete Collection
Mate Of The Werewolf
The Dangers Of Adopting A Werewolf
All I Want For Christmas Is A Werewolf

The Pleasures of His Punishment

The Pleasures of His Punishment: The Complete Collection
The Billionaire Next Door
The Millionaire and the Librarian
Riding with the Cop
Secret Desires of the Counselor
In Trouble with the Boss
Rough Ride with a Cowboy
Rough Day for the Teacher
A Forfeit for a Cowboy
Just what the Doctor Ordered
Wicked Romance of a Vampire

The Curve Collection: Big Girls and Bad Boys Series

The Curve Collection: The Complete Collection
The Curve Ball
The Beast Loves Curves
Curves by Design

BOOKS BY CALI MACKAY

The Blackthorn Brothers Series

Forced
Shattered
Vengeance
Scorch

The Billionaire's Seduction Series

Passion
Obsession
Scandal
Temptation

The Billionaire's Temptation Series

Seduction and Surrender
Submission and Surrender
Love and Surrender
Deception and Surrender
Ravage and Surrender

Forbidden – The Townsend Twins Series

Part 1 – 4
Also available as a box set

The Silver Moon Pack Series

Greyson
Part 1 - 4
Also available as a box set

Made in the USA
Coppell, TX
23 January 2023

11534901R00099